A Girl and Her Demon

by

Jon Fabris

CHAPTER 1

The smog hung over Rathberg like a soggy gray blanket. It was dusk, and Millicent had just woken up. She despised the daytime even though its harsh, bright sun seldom penetrated the coal and wood smoke that smothered the city. Nighttime was more exciting – when unexpected things could and did happen - when the urchins, drunks, prostitutes, and thieves took over the streets.

She opened her window and listened to the buzz of the city down below: shouting and cursing of all manner, clopping of horses on the cobblestones, creaking of carriage wheels, glass breaking, the far-off whistle of a train, dogs barking, laughter, music coming from a dozen sources.

The Clockwork Spire, rising into the sky like a dagger, announced the hour with a dull ringing.

The wyvern flocks were beginning to take flight, their dark shapes weaving between the towers, creating enchanting silhouettes against the darkening sky. These creatures were not vermin; they were tolerated and even beloved by some as mascots of the city. The size of a cat, with leathery wings like a tiny dragon, rarely attacked a living human and provided the valuable service of cleaning the streets of trash, vermin, and carrion.

She addressed herself in the full-length, silver gilt mirror. Four-foot-ten, with curly blonde hair and a flawless peaches and cream complexion, she scowled at the girl standing before her. For a moment, she considered dying her hair black and making her eyes look dark, but then she changed her mind and decided she was happy with her appearance.

This was a special day—her fifteenth birthday —and today, her father promised he would finally let her summon a demon to be her familiar. This privilege was reserved for the aristocracy and only those with the talent and skill to command magic. As the daughter of the Minister of Magic, she was allowed this favor.

She picked a red ribbon from her dresser and tied back her hair. Then, she put on a white dress but remembered she had to go outside tonight and be wary of the ever-present soot, so she put on a black one with her black boots. She took a stiletto out of her dresser, pressed the button that popped the blade out, and admired it momentarily. It was a present from her father on her thirteenth birthday; it had a bone handle inlaid with her initials in gold, and the blade was steel and had lovely blood grooves. She put it in a secret pocket in her dress, hoping she would get an opportunity to use it tonight.

She skipped the four flights down her private stairwell two steps at a time and emerged into the waiting hall, the walls and floor richly adorned with black marble. White marble was inlaid in the center of the room in the shape of a raven next to a crescent moon - the family crest. A towering man of middle age with gray but thick hair and a formidable mustache and beard stood guard at the bottom of a broad stairway that led up to her father's chambers.

"Good evening, Millicent. Happy birthday," he said in his gruff, soldierly way.

"Thank you, Cerberus. I'm going to High Street for some things."

"Would you like me to escort you?"

"No." She giggled.

"Stay out of trouble," he said as she passed through the door into the night.

She walked a few blocks along the busy but not too crowded streets, gas lamps lighting the way. Taking a shortcut, she turned into a dark alley, and a couple of men skulking against a wall leered at her, which she ignored. Her face was set in a perpetual innocent smirk, and she paid him no heed. It got quiet, and she sensed danger, nervous anticipation building in her breast. From out of a dark nook stepped a man, shabbily dressed, his eyes glazed from either drugs or madness.

Saying nothing, he lunged at her, grabbing.

She quickly stepped back, drew her stiletto, and brandished it in his face. Self-preservation won out over whatever mayhem the man had in mind, and he ran off. She put her knife back and continued, emerging from the alley into High Street, bustling with activity. Fine shops of every kind lined both sides of the street. Passing a dressmaker, she admired the pink Princess Line gown momentarily, then continued down the street.

She encountered an urchin sitting against a building, her face solemn and eyes distant. Millicent bent down and gave her a ducat, laughing at how her eyes lit up when she saw the gleaming gold in her palm.

There was a commotion at the haberdashery just up the road; a group was crowded at the window looking in. Millicent elbowed her way to the front to see. In the shop window was a dead man, sitting on a chair, smartly dressed and wearing a fine hat. Staring at it with fascination, she overheard enough chatter from the crowd to deduce that he was a killer recently hanged. For whatever reason, the shopkeeper bought the corpse, had it embalmed, and displayed it in his window. Odd, but if they wanted attention, it seemed to work.

She continued, stopping at a wooden sign with a mortar and pestle engraved in black, and stepped inside. Breathing deeply, she enjoyed the rich aroma of a thousand different spices, herbs, reagents, balms, perfumes, essential oils, and dried things of all kinds, known and unknown. Lining the walls and along a few aisles were dusty wooden shelves filled with bottles, jars, boxes, and bags of every conceivable color, shape, and size. The shop-keep was nowhere to be seen, but she heard snoring and followed the sound, finding him in a chair in one of the aisles, fast asleep. He was a small, slightly portly man with gray whiskers sticking out like a rodent and dressed in a gray work suit.

She smiled, then shrieked so loud and shrill that even people passing outside were startled. The shopkeeper screamed and fell off his chair, causing some brown powder in a bag on one of the shelves to burst and spill onto his shoulder. Millicent laughed heartily.

"Damnit, Millicent, you bitch! I'm too old for jokes like that."

"If you could only have seen yourself," she blurted out between gusts of laughter.

He walked behind the counter, scowling, opened a tiny jar, took out a spoonful of white powder, and snuffed it. Regaining his composure, he said calmly, "Now, young lady -" (there was an element of irony in his pronouncement of the word 'lady'), "what type of poison do you need tonight? Or will it be some sort of explosive?"

"I'm summoning a demon tonight!" she exclaimed ebulliently. Her smile faded when he showed no reaction.

"You'll be needing some sulfur then," he said dryly.

"And a score of black candles," she said with less enthusiasm.

"Size?"

"What?"

"What size candles?"

"Oh. Piccola," she said with an exaggerated foreign accent.

"Anything else?"

"A small bottle with a stopper. You could at least show some vim. It is my birthday, you know," she said petulantly, arms crossed.

He grunted in response as he measured a pound of sulfur into a leather bag, then took out the candles and wrapped them in paper.

"Oh, and some bat hairs, mercuric-nitric acid crystals, mandrake root, and a small vial."

He scowled at her silently for a moment. She grinned sweetly back. He sighed and began climbing a creaky wooden ladder to reach a top shelf. He grabbed something, slowly came back down, then walked to the end of the counter and grabbed something from another shelf, placing these into a small canvas bag.

"23 ducats."

She took out a small purse, counted eight large and three small coins, and placed them on the table.

He handed over the package, and she turned to leave.

"Wait," he said gruffly.

Bending down under his counter, he searched for something momentarily, then popped back up. He handed Millicent an amulet made of obsidian carved into the shape of a raven - her house sigil.

"For your birthday, it will bring you good luck," he said, his voice losing some but not all of its monotone.

She placed it around her neck, smiled, and said, "Thank you, Hieronymus!" and rushed out the door.

There was one last thing she needed, and it would take some care. She walked for a time, thinking and watching, then came to a theater and was inspired to enter. The show was nearing the end, and the ticket taker ignored her, reading some paper. She passed through a curtain and looked into the theater.

The stage was decorated with marble columns, and a man dressed in white robes was reciting dialogue. The play took place in ancient times. It was very dull, and she looked around at the audience, but it was too dark to see any faces. A crow (fake) flew down and landed on the stage in front of the man. The audience gasped; it was supposed to be some kind of omen. Then, another man in robes ran over, and they argued, and the second man stabbed the first, and then more men came and stabbed the first man more. It was meant to be some insurrection that happened in ancient times, but she couldn't remember the story, history not being her strong suit. There was blood, but Millicent could tell it was not real, so she was not impressed, but the audience applauded enthusiastically.

People started to file out, and she stood out of the way by the wall, watching. She picked out one man; tall, in good physical condition, obviously well-bred and wealthy from his fine clothing, and quite suitable for her purposes. He was with two other men who seemed subordinate. They spoke briefly in the foyer, then exited to the street, and Millicent followed. After a few blocks, the two other men tipped their hats farewell and turned down a different road while she followed the tall man.

They passed into a quieter, more exclusive district of the city, with wide streets lined with stately trees and large estates built of brick and stone.

She followed for a few more blocks until no others were on the street, then began walking more quickly to catch up.

He turned to climb the landing to a building, a fine estate built of pink sandstone.

Thinking quickly, she fell and loudly said, "Ow."

The man turned and looked at her for a moment.

She grabbed her ankle and moaned as if she were in great pain.

"Can I help you, young lady?"

"Please," she answered.

He came to her and stooped down. "Do you live far away?"

She looked up at him, saying nothing, pretending to be in great pain.

He picked her up, arms under her legs and back.

"You can stay in my suite while you recover. I will fetch a carriage to take you home." His voice was deep, but he looked more youthful close-up than she thought.

He carried her inside to a dark antechamber, well furnished and opulent.

As soon as he closed the door behind him, she smiled and stabbed him in the heart with her stiletto. He dropped her, staggered for a few steps, then collapsed, his life's blood spilling out. Quickly, she took out an empty vial and filled it with the blood that was oozing rapidly out of the wound in his chest. When it was full, she stoppered it and took a moment to look around. The room was richly decorated; the man was wealthy. That was good; his blood would attract a more powerful demon. She was tempted to explore the house but knew the summoning must happen when the blood was still fresh, so she started to leave. Passing by a pretty little figurine of a crow on a table, she snatched it up impulsively and exited, so excited that she ran all the way home.

She ran past Cerberus without a word and back up the stairwell, passing the door to her rooms and continuing up to the top floor. Past the door was a large open chamber with glass in the ceiling shaped like a starburst, through which the sky could be seen. This high up, the smog would occasionally be clear enough to reveal stars and the moons. She ran to a loft positioned along one of the walls and called up. "Nicodemus! Are you up there?"

Nicodemus was her magic tutor. He had once taught her father and was one of the city's premiere instructors, but he had fallen on hard times, and now he was old and retired and was content to tutor only Millicent. Her father was generous, and she was an excellent student, if undisciplined.

He taught her much of what she knew about magic and the five major disciplines. Abjuration – the study of protective magic and defensive wards and charms. Conjuration is the act of summoning or manifesting objects, entities, or energies. Divination involves seeking knowledge by scrying or reading the stars, tea leaves, entrails, and such to gain insight into the future. This was Millicent's least favorite. Enchantment and Illusion were two disciplines grouped because of their similarity. Illusion was the creation of sights or sounds through sensory manipulation or cognitive distortion, while enchantment was the act of controlling another's mind. Transmutation is the art of changing matter into different forms. Finally, there was Evocation, which was magic that utilized the forces of nature. There was another discipline called Necromancy, but it was strictly forbidden by the Magic Ministry, and those who dabbled in it would be punished severely. Nicodemus would never speak of it despite Millicent often pestering him about it. Just mentioning the subject would put the tutor into a foul mood and result in a severe reprimand.

"Nicodemus!" she called louder.

"Huh! What is it?" An ancient and sleepy voice called back down.

"It's my birthday! Did you forget!? I'm to summon my demon."

"Blood and fire," he cursed. "Did you remember to apply for the summoning from the committee." He sounded tired.

In Rathberg, the summoning of demons was strictly regulated by the Magic Ministry, and overseen by a special committee of Mages. The blood sacrifices were always taken from condemned men.

"My father is the Minister of Magic, silly, no need for all that."

"Mitra help me! Where did you get the blood? Ah! I take no blame for this. If they find out, I am not responsible!"

"Calm down, the man will not be missed."

"Have you all the materials?" He was beginning

to calm slightly, resigned to the situation.

She nodded and murmured an affirmative.

"The sulphur?"

"Yes," she answered impatiently.

"Very well." Nicodemus appeared. He was tiny and ancient, with long white hair and joints that clicked as he descended the ladder but climbed surprisingly spritely for one so old.

Following his instructions, she carefully traced a large circle on the floor with the salt, then a pentacle inside the circle, and placed a candle on each point. In the center was a pile of hot coals on which sat a brass brazier. She put the sulfur, bat hairs, mercuric-nitric acid crystals, and a piece of the mandrake root in the brazier. The contents of the brazier began to smoke, and the foul odor of brimstone arose.

"Now, add the blood," said Nicodemus; there was tension in his voice.

She unstoppered the little vial and poured it into the brazier. Immediately, it hissed and began smoking.

"Come back outside the pentagram, you fool!" he shouted.

She daintily jumped back outside of the magic circle and watched the smoke gather, becoming unnaturally dark, blacker than black.

"Now speak the incantation like I taught you."

She began speaking in an ancient language now

used only for magic. The incantation took a minute to complete and had to be recited perfectly, with specific inflections on certain words.

The air bristled with magic. She felt slightly lightheaded. This was the most powerful spell she had ever cast, and it drained her more than she had expected.

"What now?" Her heart was pounding with excitement.

"Now we can only wait and see what manner of demon is attracted by your offering, if any. No matter what happens, do not enter the pentagram, not until it tells you its name," he whispered gravely.

Minutes passed, and the smoke increased in volume, almost filling the area inside the pentagram but not escaping outside. The room became cold, so much so that frost appeared with her breathing. The foul odor of brimstone filled her nostrils with each breath.

"Why is it taking so long?" she asked impatiently.

"You found a suitable sacrifice?" he accused.

"Yes! He was young and fit, and rich and powerful," she insisted.

"Behold!" he shouted, pointing with a trembling finger.

A shape began to coalesce within the smoke, a biped, about four feet tall, the smoke slowly dissipating as it formed.

Eyes wide, she smiled with anticipation as it slowly coalesced. Her smile faded as the creature completely materialized.

It looked like a cross between a human and a pig, standing on two legs with pallid pinkish skin. Pudgy, it had rolls of fat underneath wisps of coarse white fur. The face was hideous in its asymmetry, yet at the same time, it was not particularly scary-looking.

Her brow furrowed in disappointment, and she looked back at Nicodemus, "Can I send it back?"

"What? No. Don't be foolish."

"It's just so... Unimpressive."

"Get on with the ceremony before it escapes," he ordered.

"What is your name demon?"

It looked around, confused, as if not knowing where it was.

"Tell me your name!" she commanded.

"Let me out!" it said in a voice pitched surprisingly high and exceedingly unpleasant but not at all frightening or what she would consider demonic.

She glared at Nicodemus. He glared back.

"Not until you tell me your name!" she said.

There was a pause of several heartbeats, "Zarblerg," it said.

"Speak the ritual," Nicodemus commanded.

"Zarblerg, by the laws of blood and fire, you will obey me for as long as I breathe, and do everything in your power to prevent me from coming to harm," She intoned.

"I will obey," it said after a slight hesitation.

She put out all five candles, scrutinizing the demon as she circumnavigated it, and the connection to the underworld was cut.

"Now, Zarblerg, what powers do you possess?" she asked eagerly.

"Mistress?"

"How can you serve me? What spells can you cast? Can you belch fire? Turn my enemies to stone with your gaze? Spit poison?"

"I can become invisible. I can leave this plane and exist in the ether."

"Is that all?!"

"Yes."

"Leave us, Zarblerg. Return when I summon you." She was furious.

"Mistress." He disappeared.

"What happened? Are you sure we did it right? That is the most pathetic demon I've ever seen," she whined.

"Yes, I am sure. The demon summoned cannot be predicted. The more powerful demons are attracted by more powerful and vital blood sacrifices. Are you sure the man you took the blood from was not old and feeble?"

"Yes!"

"Strange, It does indeed seem to be a lesser demon, but these things are difficult to predict. It is just as well; you are young; after all, a powerful demon is difficult to control. Your father must be mad, allowing a young girl to summon her own demon. I don't know, sometimes I think-"

"Can I send it back and find a better one."

"What? No! It doesn't work that way. Demons can be banished, of course, but if you attempted to summon another one, it is unlikely any will come."

"Bollocks!" she exclaimed, stormed off, kicking over the brazier, and returned to her rooms. When she changed into her nightgown, she realized the raven necklace given to her by Hieronymus was gone. She must have dropped it in the struggle with the man she stabbed. This made her even more upset, surely it was a bad omen. Perhaps that was why her summoning went badly.

CHAPTER 2

In bed she stayed for several days, brooding and sulking in her darkened room, seeing no one. Servants left food at her door, which she barely picked at.

After the third day, a loud and commanding knock shook her door.

"Begone! I am dreadfully crapulous!"

Another knock.

"Mollami!"

Another.

"I said, go away! Are you stupid?"

"Millicent. Your father has summoned you. I am to give you something," Cerberus said.

She got up from her bed, slowly walked to the door, and opened it.

Her hair was frazzled and unwashed.

Cerberus held up to her a sealed envelope.

"What is it?" she asked eagerly, curiosity driving away her sadness.

"An invitation to the City Moon Gala."

Immediately, she snatched it, smiling, her eyes lighting up with excitement.

She looked at the envelope.

"Tomorrow night!" he said as she slammed the door shut as if she forgot Cerberus was there.

He shouted from the other side of the door, "Your father reminds you to be on your best behavior and not to make him regret the invitation."

"Yes, yes," she answered.

She opened the envelope and read.

Millicent of the House of Ravens,

Your illustrious presence is requested
at the Moons Masquerade Gala.

Twin Plenilune, Dusk

Ophidian Hall

*no demons, imps, or familiars allowed

The Moons Masquerade Gala was a fete held on the night of the double full moons, which occurred approximately every other year. It was the first time her father had allowed Millicent to attend the fete. The most important people in Rathberg attend, and he no doubt feared she would embarrass him.

"Best behavior indeed!" she muttered to herself. "Just because I like to be seen and noticed and not skulk in the shadows." She rolled over on her bed, thinking about what she would wear.

An urge to tell someone the news came over her, and she sat up, intending to climb to the tower to Nicodemus, but then changed her mind, thinking his sour attitude would spoil her mood. Another idea occurred to her.

"Zarblerg," she said.

In a moment, her familiar appeared in a foul-smelling poof of smoke.

"I was invited to the Moon Gala!"

Its ugly face registered nothing.

"It's the most important gathering in the city. All the ministers, directors, guild masters, and most important mages will all be there."

Still nothing.

Exasperated, she continued, "Well, say something, you hideous thing."

"I don't understand, mistress," it said.

"Great donkey balls, you are stupid. Very well, allow me to educate you, sit."

The demon sat on the ground as bidden, and she began to recount the history of the city: the revolution two hundred years ago, which expelled the nobility and converted the kingdom into an oligarchy ruled by a collection of ministers, the names of its most powerful ruling houses, the creation and recent elevation of the Tech Ministry, and even some of the latest gossip. She spoke for hours until her throat became sore and her voice hoarse.

"Now then, do you understand why I am excited?"

"Yes, you seek to elevate your status and become more powerful. I share this desire."

"You are a lesser demon, aren't you? Are you considered an imp? Why did you answer my summoning and not a more powerful demon?"

"None of my brethren would answer an incomplete blood sacrifice. I alone-"

"What do you mean incomplete blood sacrifice!?"

"The blood was from a human that still lives in this plane."

"Still lives! Impossible, I stabbed him in the heart." She crossed her arms petulantly. "So it is my fault I got you."

"My brothers would have sought to betray you and escape. I will be loyal," it said eagerly.

"Well, that's something at least. You may go now, Zarblerg."

"Mistress," it said and vanished.

For a moment, she almost felt sorry for the creature but quickly shook it off. She prided herself on her mental discipline. It was one of the fundamental lessons her father, Lucian, and her tutors instilled in her. Now drowsy, she pulled over her comforter and fell quickly asleep.

CHAPTER 3

Before the death of her mother, Annabelle, when she was an infant, Lucian barely saw or paid any attention to his daughter. But after a few years, when it was evident that he would never have a son or another heir, he took great pains to educate her, hiring the best tutors in every subject a young elite woman could need. She was a quick learner in almost every subject; math, geography, languages, writing, and magic. However, she stubbornly neglected studies in the traditionally feminine subjects that didn't interest her, such as music, painting, poetry, and most of the arts. Wanting to prepare her for the often Machiavellian world of upper-class Rathberg, he also ensured she was instructed in the disciplines of self-defense, hand-to-hand combat, swordsmanship, archery, etc. Her first love, however, seemed to be The Art, and he saw an uncommon magical talent in her. Although female Ministers and Directors were unusual, they were not unheard of, and he hoped that, with careful preparation, she would be able to succeed him in the Magic Ministry. Her main weakness was her complete lack of tact and diplomacy. Every attempt to hire a tutor to teach her any of the feminine arts was met with lawsuits, tantrums, and numerous and diverse disasters. But Lucian remained hopeful that, with time, she would mellow.

This fatherly attention was mainly invisible to her; in fact, he paid very little direct attention to her. He was very busy with his duties, and to be truthful, he didn't know how to relate to a young girl. They did play games and solve puzzles together, but there was little conversation and even less overt affection, but that was the norm in upper-class Rathberg society.

When Millicent was ten, her father sent her out across town to purchase a book he needed for a spell. Halfway there, on a street without any people, she was accosted by a vagabond. In fact, it was her father be-spelled with illusion. The vagabond lurched out from a doorway and grabbed her from behind with rough, calloused hands. She handled it splendidly, her training immediately kicking in, and quick as a snake, she wriggled out of his grasp. For extra measure, she kicked him in the privates, then in the head when he bent over, then ran swiftly away.

Lucian aimed to test her mettle, but he mostly wanted to ensure she would not panic and forget all her self-defense training. The test was a success, but for his trouble, he got a mild concussion, a contusion in his testicles, and numerous bruises.

It was the first time Millicent faced an actual attacker, or so she thought at the time. Her feelings were mixed. Partly, she was truly traumatized and had nightmares for many weeks afterward, and triggered a lifelong hatred for vagabonds. Yet, she also found the experience exhilarating and empowering.

This incident went a long way toward assuaging Lucian's fears of her enduring the challenges ahead, although he was concerned that she lacked the discipline to be a Minister or anyone of rank in the Ministry, for that matter. Lucian was more than satisfied that his daughter could fend for herself and allowed her great lenience, letting her go and do what she would, although he was truly too busy to take an active role in her rearing.

CHAPTER 4

On the night of Millicent's summoning, Deputy Director Aldebrand of the Justice Ministry left the theater with his assistant Gumarich and an undersecretary from the Ministry of Tech. He seldom attended the theater, thinking it was frivolous, but this was an opportunity to connect with a man from the Tech Ministry, which could help him in his career. Rising to the rank of deputy director at such a young age was impressive for someone from a minor house, but he had much greater ambition: to be the youngest minister in Rathberg's history. On his walk home, he was consumed with thought; during the meeting, he learned of momentous events at play and had to tread carefully.

After unlocking the door to his estate, he heard a sound behind him on the street. A young girl had collapsed. She was dressed well and definitely not a beggar, so he rushed to help her. She seemed out of her senses and couldn't speak, so he picked her up and carried her into his estate, intending to give her a potion to revive her. Immediately after stepping inside, he felt a sharp pain in his chest and saw blood. The girl held a knife and laughed like a madwoman. Dropping her, he collapsed and blacked out.

The moons favored Aldebrand that night because, moments after being stabbed and left for dead, Gumarich appeared at his door, wanting to give him a paper handed to him by the man he walked with after parting with his superior. Luckily, he knew where Aldebrand kept an emergency healing potion and quickly treated the victim, his quick action no doubt narrowly saving the life of his superior from a mortal wound.

As he recovered, Aldebrand pondered the incident, trying to determine its purpose. Assassinations were not uncommon in Rathberg, but the Assassins Guild didn't recruit young girls, at least not that he knew of. His crow figurine was missing, and he wondered if robbery was the motive. The trinket was not valuable, and nothing else was missing, but there was gold and silver in the house.

He examined the scene of the crime closely and noticed a small necklace of a raven carved out of obsidian on the floor by the door. The raven was the house sigil of the Magic Minister. Perhaps it was an assassination attempt after all, or a warning. He smiled; soon, he would have his revenge.

CHAPTER 5

Millicent spent half the day at the salon, having her hair done up into a mass at the top of her head with curly golden ringlets spilling past her ears and cheeks. The choice of her dress was made during the previous fretful night. It was Robin's egg blue, fitting tight at the neck and breast but billowing at her waist. The style was of a bygone age, and she knew it would generate much attention. Her makeup, as was her style, was minimal, with just a little eyeliner. The mask she chose was of a raven, made of shiny black porcelain, in honor of her house.

At last, nighttime came, and she waited impatiently for her father to escort her to the fete, primping and scrutinizing herself in the mirror. She frowned, then smiled and ran to her dresser. Rummaging through a drawer, she pulled out a necklace of a large, rather grotesque spider, all in shiny black metal. Exactly what she needed, she thought to herself after putting it on.

A knock came on her door, and she rushed to open it, scowling when she saw Cerberus there.

"Your father was unexpectedly delayed and will

meet you at the gala. I am to escort you there."

Millicent hid her disappointment and said, "Let's go then."

The gala was at the Ophidian Tower in the center of town; it was one of the oldest and grandest towers in the city. Millicent's carriage arrived, and Cerberus stepped out and offered his hand to help her down. A few guests lingered about the entrance talking, while some walked inside past the two guards dressed in their ceremonial best at the massive double doors, which remained propped open. Cerberus walked her to the door. She showed the invitation to one of the guards and entered alone.

A long, wide hallway funneled guests into a vast auditorium, wide and very long, with a ceiling as tall as the tallest tree. Along the sides were long tables filled with sumptuous drinks and food of all varieties, and servants were standing at attention to portion the victuals. The servants were intended to be invisible, dressed plainly in black and wearing plain, full white masks covering their entire faces. At the far end was a small orchestra playing polite background music; no one was dancing. At the other end of the hall was a large fountain carved of granite, taller than a horse, which sparkled in a pinkish color. Coming closer, she saw glasses stacked like a pyramid and saw people filling them with what was in the fountain. Her eyes widened in amazement; it was filled with sparkling wine.

She studied the crowd. It was mostly old people in very drab clothing, almost exclusively black and gray. The masks were all black half-masks, mainly covering the eyes and leaving the mouth free for talking, eating, and drinking. People were gathered in clutches of two to five, conversing. As she passed, she noticed many people staring at her, the men astonished and the women scowling in outrage, muttering to each other in tones of disgust. Polite, upper-class Rathbergians praised austerity in their dress, especially at a formal and sacred event, especially by young women, who were meant to be demure and unostentatious. Millicent giggled to herself, pleased.

A young man wearing a bat mask approached her and bowed, "Secretary Ballimore at your service."

She offered him her hand, which he kissed. "Millicent, of the House of Ravens."

His eyebrows rose, indicating he was impressed. "So, your father is Minister Lucian?"

"Yes," she said absently, her eyes scanning the crowd.

"I am honored. Is this your first Moon Gala?"

"Indeed."

"What is your impression?"

"It is rather more fusty than I expected; why is no one laughing?" Her brow furrowed behind her mask.

He smiled. "Your candor is charming and most

refreshing, but I agree, it is rather stuffy, but if you observe carefully, you will find some entertainment. Look there." He turned his head discreetly; she also looked. "Minister Loque, speaking to that attractive woman who is not his wife, they are having a torrid affair, and behind her husband watching, jealousy burning in his eyes. And there," he nodded towards a group of two young men and a few young ladies. "Men from the Tech Ministry, trying to seduce those ladies. See how bored they are? Women hate tech, can't understand it."

Millicent grinned.

"Ah, behold, your father arrives."

She turned and saw her father enter the hall briskly, dressed in a simple black suit and a plain black mask, two attendants at his flanks. He spotted her and approached.

"Millicent," he said without much warmth.

"Father," she answered, copying his deep monotone. He did not appear to notice; he seemed distracted.

"Forgive my tardiness; there was an important matter I had to attend to." His gaze regarded her companion.

"Father, do you know Secretary Ballimore? He was revealing some delicious gossip," she said, grinning.

Ballimore looked shocked at her confession, and his face reddened as they shook hands.

"Ballimore, I have heard good things about you."

"Thank you, Minister," fawned Ballimore.

Another man approached and greeted the Minister, who then introduced him to his daughter. This happened repeatedly, and Millicent became bored. When her father's head was turned, she took the opportunity to slip away quietly and examine one of the refreshment tables.

"Millicent," a girl from behind her said.

She spun around and said, "Oh, hello Petrina." Petrina was a little older than her, much taller, skinny, and dark as a raven. She was the daughter of the Undersecretary of Records.

"This is your first Gala, is it not?" said Petrina.

"Yes."

"Well, what do you think?"

"It's rather stuffy isn't it?" replied Millicent.

"Yes, indeed. Come, I have something that will spice it up." Petrina grabbed her hand and led her to the toilet room.

Inside one of the stalls, Petrina produced a small vial and drank a sip of the red liquid.

"What is it?"

"Here, drink it. It will make the night infinitely more interesting."

Millicent hesitantly drank the syrupy liquid that burned her throat.

"I don't feel anything," Millicent said as they left the toilet room.

"Just give it a few minutes. Oh!" Petrina spotted a boy across the room. "I'm going home with him tonight if I have to... Say, do you know any love spells?"

"No," Millicent giggled.

"Pity. Tah-tah." Petrina strutted off.

Millicent wandered across the room and felt a little lightheaded, but happy.

She spied a boy she knew and saw the opportunity to have some sport with him. He was about her age but much more naive, being the sheltered son of a secretary from the Culture Ministry. She approached quietly, and when close enough to breathe on him, she whispered, "Jedebiah-"

He jumped and spun around in surprise.

She continued, "I heard some girls talking about you tonight. They said they wanted to come to your room, tie you down, and ravage you."

He turned the same color as the salmon on his plate, and his eyes bulged.

She waited for him to speak, but he appeared to have lost that ability. "Well, they were very pretty, and I think you should let them."

He continued to look terrified but then blurted out, "My father wouldn't allow it," and rushed off.

Aldebrand was engaged in conversation with his assistant Gumarich when a flash of color distracted him. He stared, and his eyes widened. "That girl."

Gumarich turned. "The one in blue?"

"Yes."

"She is like a robin in a house of ravens, pretty though," said Gumarich.

"I think it is she who stabbed me," Aldebrand said.

"Incredible. That is the daughter of Minister Lucian."

"Is she now?" said Aldebrand.

"So it was an assassination attempt!" said Gumarich.

"Perhaps," said Aldebrand in a cold and calculating tone.

"What are you going to do?"

"What can I do, indeed?"

A tall man approached, whom she ignored, fascinated by two cakes elaborately decorated like the moons Mitra and Petra, craters and all.

"Good evening," he said.

She turned and smiled, "Good evening."

He examined her for a moment.

"I am Director Aldebrand, of the Justice Ministry," he said, watching her response carefully.

"Millicent, of the House of Ravens," she said absently. In truth, she was becoming bored with the party and made only a mild attempt at being charming.

"Enchanted," he said, bowing slightly.

A fat man approached and took three portions of cake.

"That was Director Porcine, of the Ministry of Overeating," Aldebrand joked.

Millicent giggled, and a shiver ran down his spine. He was now sure this was the girl that stabbed him. He hid his shocked reaction well and said calmly, "Have a good evening."

Aldebrand returned to Gumarich, "She had no idea who I was."

"But why then?" Gumarich asked.

"Perhaps she needed my blood for a spell, but selected me randomly."

"You must be careful, if that is true you are in great danger. There is no telling what they would do with your blood. Perhaps you should visit an Abjurer," Gumarich said.

"No, it is too risky."

"Perhaps we should delay our plans," said Gumarich.

"Don't worry, my friend, soon it won't matter." Aldebrand smiled confidently.

Something about that voice sounded familiar.

Millicent watched him leave. *Was it he, the one I stabbed? She could not be sure. Did he recognize me? He only saw me briefly in the dark, and I am wearing a mask. He did seem to stare. What could he do? He may suspect, but there was no way to prove it. Oh, why did I have to stab such an important man?*

The potion began taking effect, and her heart was pounding in her chest like a team of galloping horses. Sweat started forming on her forehead, and she felt a little nauseous.

She decided to leave. Her father was in a large group of people, so she left without saying goodbye, practically running for the door.

Millicent's sleep that night was restless. She reviewed the incident with Director Aldebrand in her mind repeatedly, trying to remember what he looked and sounded like. When she did sleep, she was tormented by vivid and frightening dreams.

CHAPTER 6

Morning came, and the previous night seemed more like a nightmare than reality. She felt better, managing to talk herself into the notion that even if he recognized her, her position would put her beyond his reach.

It was a beautiful day, with the sun occasionally poking through the clouds and smog, and she decided to take the demon out to the park for a walk. She wore a black corset, black pants, and a red and black blouse and held a gay yellow parasol. She stopped at a shop and bought a diamond-studded collar and a leather leash. Many people were out enjoying the day, and she hoped to shock some people as magicians didn't usually take their demons out in public, especially not during the day.

"Zarblerg," she said to summon the demon.

The demon appeared with a flatulent pop.

"Mistress."

"Here, let me put this on you." She put on the collar while he stood there docilely.

They strolled down the path, her in the lead,

twirling her parasol and smiling at passersby. Many people were out strolling, sitting on benches or blankets with picnics, children playing and running, and couples kissing. When people saw her demon, most stared and gave her a wide berth, which she pretended to ignore but enjoyed immensely.

They passed by an old woman walking with a tiny white dog. When the dog saw Zarblerg, it began barking ferociously and pulling at the end of its leash while its owner struggled to hold it back. To her shock and embarrassment, Zarblerg started to make a sound like a fearful whine and darted to the side of Millicent, keeping her between it and the dog.

"Zarblerg, you may go!" she shouted, and it disappeared with a pop.

"You shouldn't be out here in the park with your demon; there are children and pets around," the old woman scolded.

Millicent frowned and stomped away, throwing the leash to the ground, furious at Zarblerg for embarrassing her.

CHAPTER 7

Benedict, a rakishly handsome man of about thirty with a thin mustache and a master swordsman, watched the girl from the window approaching and felt a mixture of dread and anxiety. It was his pupil, Millicent, dressed in an expensive and perfectly tailored fencing outfit made of thick white cotton. Despite her youth and short reach, she was an excellent fencer, thanks to his tutelage, good enough to occasionally penetrate his defenses and deal him a vicious jab or slash. What's worse, she was the daughter of a very important man in government, so he dared not fight too hard and risk hurting her. He took a generous gulp from his flask.

Benedict ran a school, mostly for the children of aristocrats. He taught hand-to-hand combat, archery, and especially swordplay in the large room below his bedroom.

He opened the door to Millicent, and she entered scowling; without a word, she seemed in a particularly foul mood. She wanted to fence today, but they used wooden swords for safety. Not for hers, for his. During the hour-long lesson she penetrated his defenses several times with reckless swings and dealt him some vicious bruises.

After the lesson, she felt much better, almost forgetting about the day's embarrassment. A good sweat always made her more calm and content.

CHAPTER 8

The next day was the first of the month, which meant she had to spend time with her aunt Beatrix. She was ancient, prim, and stodgy as can be, and Millicent hated spending time with her, but her father insisted. Most of the time, they just sat in Beatrix's parlor, sipped tea, and played cards. This evening, however, Millicent had talked her into going to a performance by a castrati singer named Farinelli, whom she heard was divine.

The coach rolled up to the opera house – the finest in Rathberg, and an attendant opened the door and helped them down. Beatrix was well-known, being a wealthy widow from a prominent family, and people nodded at her respectfully as she walked by. The usher escorted them to one of the prime box seats. Millicent looked around; it was the cream of Rathberg society, dressed in their finest. She admired the women's dresses and made mental notes of their style. The curtain opened, and out stepped a slender, handsome man, albeit effeminate looking. The crowd applauded enthusiastically, and he began to sing.

Millicent thought Farinelli was wonderful, singing arias written for sopranos accompanied by a harpsichordist and violinist. After the show, the applause was so loud it made her ears ring.

Beatrix asked Millicent, "Would you like to go backstage and meet him?"

"Yes," she said eagerly.

Her aunt led her down to the musician's chambers and waited outside while she was given a rose and a gold ducat and allowed into the dressing room.

There was Farinelli, sitting in a makeup chair and dressed simply in a white shirt.

He took her rose and coin and said, "Oh, what a lovely girl. And such a bold and striking sense of fashion. You are the daughter of the Magic Minister, I was told?"

"Yes, Maestro," she was unusually shy, being star-struck.

"Oh, please call me Farinelli."

Just then, another man entered, dressed as a businessman. He said, "Farinelli, don't dally. We have an... Appointment with the Director's wife."

"Forgive my rude manager, Millicent, but I must bid you adieu. But here, take my card and call on me if you please." He handed her a paper card printed with his name written in an ornate script and an address.

It had been a fine evening.

Late that night, she lay on her bed examining the figurine of the crow she had stolen. She could feel it had magic in it. The carving was incredibly detailed, made out of some smooth black stone she couldn't identify. She jumped out of bed, put on a robe, and ran up to see Nicodemus. When she opened the door, she could hear his loud snoring, but she didn't care and shouted his name. After there was no answer, she repeated it louder. He woke up and started coughing.

"Nicodemus! Come down. I need your help."

"Go to bed. Can't you see I'm sleeping, you wretched girl."

"Please! It's an emergency!"

He muttered a stream of profanity as he rose out of bed and climbed down the ladder from the loft.

"Now, what is this emergency?"

"This figurine, what is it? Is it magical?"

"This is the emergency you wicked little brat!?" he exclaimed.

"Please Nicodemus, just tell me," she whined.

He muttered something under his breath, then pulled some spectacles from his pocket and examined the crow.

"It's a figurine of a crow," he said and took his glasses off.

"I know that! Is it magical?"

"How should I know?" He suddenly threw it to the ground with great force.

She glared at him, fuming.

"Well, pick it up. If it is undamaged, it is undoubtedly magical."

She picked it up and examined it closely. "I don't even see a scratch."

"Hmm, yes, probably magical."

"What does it do? How do I activate it?"

"Impossible to say. Try the library."

"Oh, you are no help!" She turned and left.

"Bah," he answered and climbed back up to his bed.

CHAPTER 9

The feeble sun was beginning to rise over Rathberg, and the city was slowly awakening. Distant horse hoofs on cobblestones echoed in the still air. The creaking and slamming of shopkeepers opening the grates that protected their wares from thieves in the night. Above this was the dull thud of Millicent banging on the gigantic doors of the Tower of Records. The doors were made of wood, carved ornately with gargoyles, stained almost black, and shined with a thick wax coating. After banging for some time, she gave up and sat in front of the doors. She took out the crow figure, caressing its smooth surface.

About an hour later, the doors finally creaked open, and Millicent walked past the attendant without a word. She entered the Hall of Records and stared at the enormous room with wide eyes. Shelves eight stories high were lined with books as far as the eye could see.

She looked around for help and saw a tiny old man with spectacles pushing a cart thrice his size, filled with books.

"You there. I need help finding a book."

He didn't respond.

Thinking him deaf, she said more loudly, "Librarian! I need help finding a book."

He stopped, looked up at her myopically, scowled, and put his finger to his lips.

"I need to find a book about magical objects. Specifically, a statue of a crow," she said more quietly.

He turned and walked off, leaving the cart. Sensing she was not following, he turned and motioned with his finger for her to follow. He led her to a room off the main chamber. Inside was a counter with a man hunched over a book so large Millicent could have worn one of its pages as a skirt. The tiny man said something to the other man, this one equally as old and frail but tall and gaunt. He squinted at her, then thumbed through the book, his dry hands scratching at the brittle parchment, causing her to shiver with grima. After a few minutes, he seemed to find what he wanted. He turned to an enormous machine behind him that looked like the insides of a clock, began turning dials, and then pulled down a brass lever. At once, what must have been several dozen gears began turning at various speeds. The tall man grabbed an oil can and began oiling the machine in certain places. After a few minutes, the machine made a metallic rat-a-tat noise, and a paper card popped out.

The man pulled a chord hanging from the ceiling, took out a cloth, and began polishing parts of the machine, ignoring Millicent.

After another few minutes, another man appeared; this one was also old but at least looked like he had a better-than-even chance of surviving the year. He grabbed the card and ambled off. Millicent followed.

He led her across the vast chamber, stopped, consulted the card, then entered one of the rows of shelves. A ladder so tall it made her dizzy to crane her head to see the top was there, and the man began climbing. He reached the top thirty feet up, got on a walkway, walked a bit, and climbed another ladder to climb even higher. Her neck was getting sore watching, so she sat down at one of the long tables and waited. Finally, the man was back down with a book bound in red leather. He handed her the book and card without a word.

She opened the book. It was called "A Compendium of Enchanted Items, volume XIV, Animal Figurines and Totems." She turned to the index and found the word crow had many citations. It took over an hour, but finally she found a page with a drawing that looked much like her crow. The item was called a gonagas; it was ancient and created by a cult of female witches that lived far to the north, on an island inhabited by the Chuktuk people. It said the figure could be brought to life with a word of power but did not mention the word or any other helpful information. She closed the book, the space between her eyebrows wrinkled in thought, then had an idea.

Getting the book about the Chuktuk language was just as arduous as the last, but she endured it and finally had the book. Not wanting to conduct any experiments with the gonagas inside the library, she discretely stuffed the book in her knapsack and made for the exit.

Ridgeview Cemetery was just north of the library and was set up on a hill, providing a good view of Rathberg. Finding a nice patch of grass away from any watching eyes, she sat down and pulled out the book and the gonagas. Eagerly, she thumbed through the book. First, she looked up the Chuktuk word for crow, then spoke it aloud. Nothing happened. She tried several more times with different tones of voice. Disappointed but not discouraged, she tested the word for bird unsuccessfully. Stubbornly, she continued, trying fly, awaken, gonagas, wing, soar, hover, arise, and many other words. The book said "word of power," but she thought it might instead be a phrase, so she tried combining two words with no luck. She threw the bird down on the ground, disheartened. The sun was now high in the sky, and her stomach began to rumble with hunger.

Absent-mindedly, she started to skim through the book, finding a section on pronunciation, but then realized she was not speaking the language correctly, so she began duplicating her efforts with the correct accent. When she spoke the word for fly, she felt a tingle of magic from the object, but it did not move or change. She pondered for a time, trying to remember her lessons on totems, and remembered how vital state of mind and visualization of what you wanted were to magic. Then she tried imagining the bird coming to life and flying, then speaking the word. Something was happening, so she kept trying.

All at once, she felt herself leaving her body and found that she was looking through very different eyes. She looked around and saw herself sitting there, seemingly asleep. Colors were incredibly vivid; she could see colors in things that were bland to humans. The angle of her sight was also wider, and she could see more than 180 degrees around at once. This was the most powerful spell she had ever experienced. She tried moving her arms and found herself in the air. Her flying was very awkward at first, but she began to get the hang of it after a while. She was having such a ball soaring higher and higher that she lost track of time, and it was starting to get dark. Panic struck her as she suddenly realized she did not know how to get back into her own body.

Landing on herself, she tried to say the power word again, but only a caw came out. Panic began to set in, and she started imagining what would happen to her sleeping body here alone in the dark and imagined living out the rest of her life as a bird. What would she eat? What would her father think? Yes, of course, her father must know how to change her back. She tried to calm herself and think. She pecked at herself, thinking that she may be awakened as if from sleep. Then she tried to imagine herself back into her body, using the same technique of visualizing that got her into the crow. So abrupt was the transformation back and so disorienting that she wondered for a moment if she was losing her mind. After a few moments of closing her eyes and calming herself, she felt better. Looking down, she saw the bird as a figurine again.

As Millicent walked home, she began to feel like herself again, but the terror of the transformation remained so intense that she wondered if she would go through with it again despite the initial enjoyment.

Millicent returned home to find one of her father's cards wedged into the door frame. It read, "Daughter, come see me tomorrow at my office." It was signed by her father's hand. This was unusual, but it usually meant he was displeased and would scold her about something. Had he found out about her stabbing Aldebrand? She slept uneasily that night, her mind going through past scoldings and all the possible punishments that could arise.

CHAPTER 10

In the morning, she lay in bed for an hour, thinking carefully about an appropriate outfit. At last, she chose a black rider's outfit with pants, a cap, and a whip, something like the coachman's but more stylish, although never something a woman would wear.

The guards at the Ministry of Magic, being new, did not recognize the daughter of the Minister and stopped her at the entrance.

"My father is the Minister, and if you don't let me pass, I'll tear your eyes out with this whip."

Surprised, the two guards looked at each other and stepped aside to let her pass.

Knowing her, the rest of the guards allowed her to pass without a word and with barely a glance. In the center of the building was a spiral stairway that wound up to the 20th floor. Its size was such that ten teams of wagons could ascend it simultaneously. Some people walked, but most cast spells that allowed them to float up or down. Millicent felt such spells were for the old and feeble and did not know it anyway, so she used her legs to ascend to the Minister's office, one floor below the top. Millicent observed the heart of the Ministry with wide eyes. Magicians, clerks, and even some demons floated and bustled about, some carrying papers, all seemingly in a hurry.

Secretary Ambrosius was of middle age. He had long, graying hair tightly bound in the back of his head and flowing down to his waist. He also had a short mustache and beard and dark but tiny eyes. "Minister?"

Lucian looked up from his desk, "Ambrosius. Welcome. Would you like a drink?"

"No, thank you, Lucian. I have received a message from Minister Tranton. It seems he would like a meeting."

"Does he now? Probably a trap. I don't trust that man; he looks like a vulture. Tell the Tech Ministry if they wish to meet; it can be here in the Tower of Magic."

"I concur," Ambrosius answered and began walking away. He stopped, remembering something, "Oh, and the envoys from Veldon would like to change our meeting venue."

"What? Why?"

"It seems they feel the Tower of Magic is too impolitic a meeting place given the current political climate. They suggested a more neutral location so as not to appear to be favoring the Magic Ministry."

Lucian replied, "if the reason for their visit is

to discuss the creation of a galvanic suppression crystal for their city, I should think that indicates favoring the Magic Ministry. Oh, very well, I assume you have vetted the location?"

"Of course, Minister."

"When is the meeting?" asked Lucian.

"Tomorrow morning," Ambrosius said, and exited.

Stopping momentarily to catch her breath, Millicent watched one of her father's men walk by and nod to her.

She didn't know his name but didn't trust him with his little black eyes like a rat.

She walked into the office of the Minister's private secretary. He looked up from his desk and said, "Ah yes, Millicent, your father will see you now."

Lucian summoned his demon, Pythomon. He intended to send it to the meeting place to scout the location and ensure its safety, but just then, his daughter entered.

She stepped inside and was surprised to see her father with his demon. It looked like a very tall man with an elaborate rack of horns on its head, a triangle-shaped face with large eyes, and a small mouth with long fangs. Millicent only saw it a handful of times, as her father seemed to summon him seldom and only when alone.

"Father." She nodded respectfully.

"Daughter," he said. "You may go, Pythomon." The demon nodded and vanished.

Lucian sat down behind his desk, which was shaped like a huge crescent. On it were piled a multitude of papers, scrolls, and books. Millicent thought he looked tired.

"Daughter, did you enjoy the Moon Gala?"

"Yes, father, it was splendid."

"Good, good. I must speak to you about a serious matter, but you must promise not to tell anyone what I am about to say."

Millicent's heart sped up a bit; this was an exciting development. "Yes, father, I promise."

"My spies have informed me that there will be an attempt at a coup. It will fail, of course, and I have no reason to believe that you will be involved, but out of an abundance of caution, I think we should have a contingency plan. There is an abandoned castle thirty miles south of the city, on the East bank of the River Severin, named Rabe Hold. It has been in the family for hundreds of years but is in ruins. If you are in danger, Cerberus will take you there. Wait for me. You will be safe. No one will find you there. I have hidden some money and other things that you may need there, but you must use your wits to find it. I know you always loved puzzles, ever since the day you were born."

"Yes, father."

"Good. Nicodemus informed me that your demon summoning was successful?"

"Yes."

"Good, he can protect you, but be careful with it; remember your lessons."

Someone walked briskly into his office with a paper.

"Goodbye, Millicent, remember what I told you."

Walking back, the news of the coup completely left her mind; no doubt her father had the situation under control, as always. They were the most powerful house in Rathberg, nothing bad ever happened to them. Instead, her mind was consumed with thoughts of this mysterious castle she had never heard about. She daydreamed about it all the way back home. In the evening, she looked through her picture books of castles but found no mention of Rabe Hold. Strange, she had never heard about it until now.

Lucian was at his office before dawn; he had often been sleeping in an adjacent room lately, with so much work to do.

CHAPTER 11

Just past dawn, he was joined by his second in command, Balthazar, Ambrosius, and Lucian's personal secretary. The men floated slowly down the staircase to the ground floor.

"Where exactly is this meeting, Ambrosius?" asked Lucian.

"It's in a tower used by the Trade Ministry for meetings of this sort."

"Are you sure we don't need security, given the situation?" Balthazar asked.

"I think the three most powerful magicians in the city can defend themselves," answered Ambrosius.

"I wish they would openly attack rather than all this cowardly double-dealing behind our backs," Lucian said.

"Carrion do not attack; they pick at what others have killed for them," Balthazar said.

"Indeed," Lucian answered. The others chuckled.

The four men entered a coach and drove to the meeting location across town.

Doormen ushered them into the ancient building, built when ornate architecture was in vogue. They went down a hallway into a plain, empty room with a long table in the center. They took their seats.

Refreshments were on the table; wine, fruit, and bread rolls. Lucian's quick and silent spell confirmed there was no poison.

"They are late," Lucian complained.

"Shouldn't be long now," Ambrosius answered.

"Why are you sweating, Ambrosius? There were not that many stairs. Are you getting old?" Joked Balthazar.

Just then, the men felt a curious tingling sensation as a magic dampener tech machine was started in the adjacent room. It felt like all the magic was drained from the room, leaving a yawning silence. This was a shocking and terrifying event for men continuously immersed in magic. They knew that electricity could suppress magic, but were unaware that the Tech Ministry had created a machine that could so quickly and thoroughly block all magic. It was a blunder that Lucian immediately and bitterly regretted.

Lucian, instantly assessing the situation, realized his long-time friend and colleague had betrayed them. "Ambrosius, you traitor!" he shouted.

Balthazar tried to summon his demon and then cast a spell, both to no avail. Lucian knew better than even to try.

The door burst open, and eight justice officers, led by Deputy Director Aldebrand, rushed in.

"Minister Lucian, on behalf of the Justice Ministry, you are under arrest for acts traitorous to Rathberg," Aldebrand said.

"You are the traitors!" Lucian rushed the men and knocked one down with a powerful punch but was quickly overwhelmed by the rest. The secretary pulled out a knife and attacked the justice officers, who knocked him down and kept beating him until he was unconscious.

Lucian, Balthazar, and the secretary were trussed up and gagged, then dragged out to waiting justice coaches. Ambrosius remained, sweating and shaken.

Minister Tranton entered the room, walking with his hands behind his back as he often did. With his hawkish nose, deep-set eyes, and curved neck, he did indeed look like a vulture. "Congratulations, Minister, you have done well," he said to Ambrosius.

"They will not be killed?" asked Ambrosius.

"As long as they cooperate, no," Tranton said.

CHAPTER 12

Millicent was up early; it was drizzly and foggy, a perfect day for a funeral, so she took a stroll to Ridgeview Cemetery. She wore a black corseted dress of a style that only old women still wore; in fact, she stole it from her aunt. On her head was a black bonnet with a black veil, and she carried a black umbrella to complete the outfit. She stood well away from the other mourners. A young woman and a young boy were standing closest to the grave, so she inferred that the deceased was a man and a soldier because some of the mourners wore uniforms. She wondered if he died in battle and imagined several different gory scenarios, such as being impaled by a sword during a charge or perhaps crushed to death by a catapult ball. The crowd did not pay attention to her, so she cast a spell to attract some ravens, who took up perches on the tree she was standing by. It worked; people started to stare and point. Satisfied and bored, she decided to leave, conjuring some thick fog to drift before her so she could vanish into thin air.

As she strolled back to her tower, she saw five men from the Justice Ministry rushing out of the building. They looked determined and ruthless. Were they after her? Did Director Aldebrand recognize her after all? Or was this the coup? She had a moment of panic when they turned her way but stifled the overwhelming urge to run, knowing it was too late and would only attract attention to her. She hoped her disguise would protect her.

She kept walking, and they continued past her without even a glance. Not daring to go into the building, she kept walking for a few blocks until she regained her composure and turned to look back.

There was no sign of the men, so she returned and entered the building. The scene she beheld was disturbing. The floor was covered with blood, but there were no bodies or signs of Cerberus. Terribly frightened, she ran up to her room. The door was broken and hanging open. Cautiously, she peeked inside. The room was a shambles, having obviously been ransacked, although, at first glance, nothing appeared missing. She quickly gathered some things; a pouch of coins, which luckily was not taken, a change of clothes she put in a small bag, and her stiletto. On her bed, she found the crow statue; her usual mess of blankets had kept it hidden and safe.

She ran upstairs to see what happened to Nicodemus.

He was on the floor in a large puddle of blood; his glasses were gone, and his shirt was covered with blood. Millicent ran to him. His eyes were wide and filled with panic, yet he was still alive. The charred corpse of a Justice officer smoldered on the floor, the result of a spell he was able to release before he was overcome.

"Nicodemus!" she gasped, on her knees.

"Millicent. Thank the moons, I could not hold on much longer. Men from the Ministry of Justice came. Looking for you. There has been a coup. Your father killed or imprisoned, I greatly fear. Listen to me. You must go to the Harlot district and find Lucinda the Red. She will help you leave the city and be waiting for you. Go now. They will come back."

"But my aunt?"

"Probably killed too. They will capture you if you go there. Now go!"

"What's happened to Cerberus?"

"Shut up and go before it is too late." he gasped with his last breath.

"Nicodemus?" Nicodemus was gone. She stood up and stared at the body of her tutor, her body going numb.

Panic rose in her, and she ran down the stairs and through the doors. To her right, a block away, she saw some Justice men. They shouted at her.

She ran, her hat and veil flying off in the wind. She cursed the long dress she was wearing, which slowed her immensely. Turning into an alley, she heard the footfalls of the men behind her getting closer, and then she remembered her demon.

"Zarblerg!"

With a pop, he appeared. "Mistress."

"Those men are trying to kill me; stop them!"

Zarblerg turned as the men rounded the corner into the alley. There were three of them. Zarblerg began making some fierce noises, which were something between a growl and a squeal. The men stopped and drew swords. She ran, hoping the small demon could at least delay them long enough for her to escape.

She turned into a larger road. A gully was off to the side. Into it, she jumped. It was a drainage stream that ran into the sewers. She ran knee-deep in water, splashing into the sewer entrance, which was big enough for her to enter if she crouched down. Standing in the dark, gasping for breath, she tried to listen for any signs of her pursuers, but it was quiet.

She cast a spell to enhance her night vision and continued into the dark. Under the city was a warren of tunnels created from the quarries and mines from when the city was first built. During the Red Plague, cemeteries were overflowing, and the corpses were put underground by the thousands. The sewers connected to these catacombs; she knew it would be an excellent hiding place.

The tunnel she was in emptied into a larger one, tall enough to allow her to stand fully upright.

All was quiet, and she felt safe. She called for her demon.

He appeared covered with terrible gashes and cuts.

"Are you alright?!"

"Yes, I am not seriously damaged." He sounded almost cheerful.

"Good, what happened?" she said, relieved.

"I fought the men with swords; I killed one and injured another, but then they ran off."

"If I give you something, can you carry it for me?"

"Yes, mistress."

"Here," she handed it her bag. It would be easier for her to run without it.

"Now, walk on ahead of me."

"Mistress."

She stopped. "Say, could you take me with you to the place you disappear to?"

"No, mistress, I can only take small objects that do not have a soul. More powerful demons can take humans back, but the humans don't seem very happy in my plane."

"I see, never mind then," she said, and they continued on.

She came to a break in the wall, which looked like an excavation that led into the catacombs. The catacombs were dryer than the sewers, for which she was grateful. There was a wide section with some stone sarcophagi, where she took the opportunity to sit down, rest, and change her clothes. She changed into a pair of men's slacks, tunic, and boots and wrapped a cloak around her. With the hood covering her head, she could appear as a young lad and pass with less scrutiny.

She decided her next move was to wait for dark and then find Lucinda the Red as Nicodemus instructed, but first, she needed to find her way out of the catacombs; she didn't dare return the way she came.

Wandering for a while, she only seemed to get increasingly lost and began feeling scared and panicky.

"Zarblerg, can you help me find my way out of this place?"

"Mistress."

"Wait! Do you hear that?" she whispered.

It was a soft scraping sound like a snake slithering along the dirt.

She backed up and tried to go in the opposite direction of the sound, but it was too difficult to determine where it came from, and it only seemed to be getting closer.

Backing into a corner behind her demon, she drew her stiletto and waited, heart pounding.

It suddenly rounded the corner and appeared, its

appearance so hideous and evil that she screamed. It was so huge that it barely fit into the tunnel. Its hindquarters were like a slug tapering off at the end. The upper torso was raised up, and it had numerous appendages that moved continuously. The mouth was relatively small but filled with sharp teeth. The eyes were black as coal and filled with an evil intelligence.

Not only did she scream, but so did Zarblerg, who quickly vanished back into his realm.

Mad with terror, she slashed at the thing, but it kept advancing, seemingly not feeling any pain. She fell, and it continued until it was on top, smothering her. Mercifully, she blacked out.

When she awoke, she was being carried along the tunnels. The creature's grip was surprisingly soft and gentle yet firm. They came to a large chamber, so dark she could hardly see, and the creature stopped in front of a man.

The man was ancient, with long white hair and ghastly pale flesh, but his most striking feature was his white, pupil-less eyes. He scowled at her with an expression of surprise and curiosity.

He advanced and touched her face, the creature holding her steady and not letting her flinch away.

"This is curious, Adramalech; you found her in the tunnels?"

It answered with a noise but not in a language she could understand.

His hand moved down to her chest. Her legs were free, and she kicked, connecting solidly between his legs, causing him to fall backward and cry out in pain.

"A young girl, but too well-groomed and finely dressed to be an urchin," he gasped, still on the ground.

"I can speak," she said irritably, regaining some of her composure.

He stood back up. "Indeed, you can. Well then, who are you? Why are you here in the under-city?"

She wondered for a moment if she should lie but sensed that this man was not allied with her enemies, and her heritage had always caused people to treat her with respect in the past.

"I am Millicent of the House of Ravens, daughter of Lucian – Minister of Magic."

His surprise was palpable. He raised his arm and pointed a finger. "I know Lucian, and I have met you, but that was when you could not even walk. Put her down, Adramalech, gently."

She was put down and she hugged herself, and took a step away from the demon, still out of sorts from the kidnapping.

"Now, tell me, what brings you here?" he asked eagerly.

"Your slug demon is what brought me here."

"Yes, he hunts for me, but luckily for you was

wise enough to know I would want to speak to you instead of eating you."

"Yes, it's my lucky day."

"But why were you in the catacombs?"

"There was a coup, and my father was taken, probably killed. Men from the Ministry of Justice are hunting for me, trying to kill me," she said, her voice dripping with bitterness.

"I see; that is unfortunate. Is Morcant still Minister of Justice?"

"Yes."

"I knew he was ambitious, but I would never have guessed such a bold move. If they are after you, they no doubt want you as a hostage, which means your father still lives."

This surprised her and lifted her mood.

"I don't think Lucian would hide, so he must be captured. Why would they need you if they already had him," he said, facing away from her as if speaking to himself.

"I'm still here."

"Ah, I think I have it! They need something from him that he must willingly surrender, but what?"

"Where would they be keeping him?" she asked.

"Oh, somewhere in the Justice Ministry tower, no doubt."

"Who are you? How do you know these things?"

"I? I am Aldous; I was a director in the Magic Ministry," he said proudly. "How do I come to be here? You are about to ask."

"Don't care."

He ignored or didn't hear that and continued, "I was doing cutting-edge research, exploring the darkest secrets of necromancy, and a spell went terribly wrong, blinding me. Not only that, the magic I was attempting was forbidden, so I was expelled from the Ministry. After 51 years of service." He shook his head sadly. "The Justice Ministry wanted to punish me, and so I fled and now hide here, in a place where my blindness is no handicap."

She saw an opportunity and said with all the sweetness she could muster, "I am so sorry, Aldous. You have been mistreated. It seems we both have a common enemy."

"Why yes, I suppose we do."

"Perhaps... No, I shouldn't ask," she said sweetly.

"Ask what?"

"Will you help me rescue my father?" she asked with mock hesitation.

"What? You must be mad; what could I do?"

"You know things, and you have your demon," she pleaded.

He looked down and began wringing his hands.

"I have not set foot above ground in thirteen

years."

"Please. My father will be grateful and see to it that your position is restored."

He began pacing for a time, contemplating, "Your father was very kind to me. He helped me find this place. Even visited me once, took my notes. He was interested in my research, I think he saw its possibilities. Very well, I will help you," he finally said.

"Oh, thank you, Aldous!" She hugged him, feeling nothing but bones under his cloak.

"Now, none of that. To get your father out of the Justice tower is no small feat; I must make a plan. It will take time."

"How long?"

"Oh, days, perhaps weeks."

"Weeks!?" She wondered if this ancient man was too old to be of use after all.

"Yes, but you may take my bed. I can sleep in the chair; I don't sleep much anyway."

She looked over at a filthy cot along the wall. The thought of spending another night in this place horrified Millicent. "No, I have another place to stay. Can you lead me out to the surface?"

"Yes, my demon can take you. Return in a few days, and we will speak of the plan to free your father."

"Thank you, Aldous. Please hurry, he is in

danger."

The slug demon moved, and she followed for what might have been half an hour until they reached a room with an iron ladder leading up to a trap door. She climbed the ladder and, with great effort, lifted the heavy trap door, revealing a small dark room. An oblong shape was in the room, but it appeared to be deserted. She climbed up and realized she was in a crypt with a stone sarcophagus in the center.

Suddenly, Zarblerg reappeared.

"You are useless! Where did you go!?" She said furiously.

"My deepest apologies, mistress, but the demon we faced was of the highest rank, and I am forbidden to fight it."

"Horse crap! Get lost! I don't need you now."

The demon vanished.

The door to the outside was made of heavy wood and bolted from the inside. She unlocked it but could not move the heavy and rusted door.

"Zarblerg, come back and help me open this door."

He appeared and pushed the door. It slowly opened with a strident creak.

CHAPTER 13

She stepped outside and found herself in a cemetery with crypts of all shapes and sizes, primarily overgrown by trees and vines. It was evening, just after sundown.

"I know where we are, about 10 blocks from the Harlot district. Hopefully, I won't be noticed with these boys' clothes. Zarblerg, you are not inconspicuous, farti friggere!"

Zarblerg disappeared.

She pulled the hood over her head and emerged into the deserted street. As she neared the Harlot District, there were more and more people, all of the unsavory variety, but she passed without attention.

She was now in the center of the district but had no idea where to find Lucinda the Red, so she began asking people on the street. They ignored her or just stared mutely, so she went to the nearest brothel and entered. It was a small, dark, gaudy room decorated superficially elegantly. A well-dressed man greeted her with a smile.

"Good evening, lad; your first time, is it?"

"I am looking for Lucinda the Red," she said, trying to make her voice deeper.

"Hah, trust me, you don't want her. She is old enough to be your grandmother."

"That's what I want," she said, trying to get the information without speaking too much and giving herself away.

"Oh, I catch your scent, lad. We don't judge here." he said, winking knowingly, "It's good you know what you like at your age. You'll find her a few doors down; just look for the red door."

"Come back if you decide you want a fresh young filly," he said as she turned to leave.

Back on the street, she spotted the red door, and as a man rushed out, she entered, finding herself in a plainly decorated coat room.

The attendant said, "May I take your coat?"

"No," she said, passing through a red curtain into a large, dimly lit room with many couches and comfortable chairs. The place stunk of stale perfume. It was not crowded; a few men were seated with women, who were mostly topless. An older woman with unnaturally red hair took notice and approached her.

"Welcome to my home, young man. Won't you come with me?" She was led down a hallway, up some stairs, and into a room. She lit a candle and then regarded her.

"Who knows you came here?" Lucinda asked in a low voice.

"Just Nicodemus."

"Did anyone follow you?"

"No."

Lucinda seemed to relax, and her countenance softened. "You may stay here as long as you need. I will have food sent to you three times a day, but you must be quiet and stay in this room."

"But what am I to do? Do you have another room? This place is awful?"

"No, I don't! For now, just keep quiet; the entire justice force is looking for you." Lucinda scolded as she left the room.

Millicent sighed, shed her cloak and sat down on the bed. It was lumpy.

"Zarblerg."

"Yes, mistress."

She scrutinized the demon, and her brow furrowed. "Zarblerg, have you grown?"

"Yes, a little, I killed a man."

"You mean when you kill someone, you get bigger?"

"Yes, mistress, if I kill and consume them. I gain power with each soul I take."

"That's wonderful; maybe eventually you will become less of a coward."

"I hope so, mistress."

Someone knocked on the door, and she said, "Entra," she said, rolling the R.

A young woman with a painted face came in bearing a tray. She saw Zarblerg, screamed, dropped the tray, and ran out of the room.

Millicent laughed. "You better hide Zarblerg."

A few minutes later, Lucinda came in, dragging the frightened girl by the arm.

"There, you see, nothing to be afraid of," Lucinda scolded.

Millicent smiled and considered calling for Zarblerg to reappear, but she was hungry and wanted the girl to return with more water and food.

"But there was a monster," the girl insisted.

"Any more talk of monsters, and I'll have you whipped!" Lucinda said, pushing her roughly.

She reddened and bent down to clean up the broken glass and tray she had dropped. After she was finished and rushed off, Lucinda turned to Millicent, "Keep your familiar hidden, you little fool."

After the meal, her boredom was interrupted by fiddle music. It was passable, but then she heard the most marvelous soprano voice join in for a moment. *Could it be?* She thought.

Quietly opening her door, she hid behind a plant a few feet away to watch. The fiddler was a young boy dressed in poor urchin rags, hired as entertainment, but she could not see the singer, who had now stopped. There were more customers in the parlor now, and Millicent remained there, hidden, entertained by the music and the banter between the customers and whores. She found how the women acted around the men and the obviously fake way they fawned over them most degrading yet amusing.

"Who's this new one!" A man snuck up behind her and pulled her out into the open. His speech was slurred, and his eyes glazed; he was very drunk.

Millicent was stunned momentarily as all the eyes in the room turned to her. Then he began pulling her toward him for a kiss. Her self-defense training kicked in, and almost without thinking, she kicked him in the bollocks, then landed a solid right cross on his chin as he doubled over in pain. He hit the floor with a thud. There, out in the open, Millicent saw none other than Farinelli lounging on one of the couches, a wench on his lap; he was staring at her, agape.

Lucinda rushed over, grabbed her roughly, and thrust her back into her room.

"I told you to stay in your room, you little shit!" she hissed, then slammed the door.

Millicent lay on the bed, now worried that Farinelli had recognized her. She wondered if she should flee but was so exhausted by the day's events that she soon fell asleep despite the lumpy mattress.

She woke up to a commotion. A man and woman were yelling, accompanied by what sounded like furniture being thrown. She made out a few of the words spoken: "Never in my life!" (the man) and "It's not my fault!" (the woman). A door was slammed, and then things quieted down.

After a few minutes, Lucinda returned to her room.

She looked at Millicent gravely and said mildly, "It just occurred to me that young ladies of your standing are bestowed with a certain spell that prevents men in your vicinity from becoming physically aroused. Has such a spell been cast on you, my dear?" she asked casually.

"Oh yes, the Virtue Spell. That was done ages ago."

"How can the spell be broken?" she said sternly.

"I don't know; I think it just goes away when I turn nineteen."

"Do you know what this place is?" Her tone was more tense.

"Of course."

"Well, what then?" Lucinda was becoming increasingly angry.

"Men pay to screw your whores."

"Yes, and how might you expect this to happen when no one in the house can get hard?"

Millicent just shrugged.

"Great moons! Nicodemus was a friend, but this is my livelihood. Come with me." She was enraged but made a great effort to keep her voice down, resulting in a whispered yell.

Millicent was agape, taken aback by her attitude. She was not used to being spoken to in such a way, especially by the lower class.

Lucinda dragged her to a back staircase and led her up several flights of stairs into a dusty attic. There was a tattered couch, some boxes, an assortment of junk, and a small window looking out onto a rooftop, which let in some of the failing daylight.

"Hopefully, this will get you and your spell out of range."

"I can't stay here, it's filthy!"

"Tough titties!" she shouted and closed the door, locking it behind her.

Millicent gestured at the door and said, "Vaffanculo!"

Even though she could easily pick the lock, Millicent decided to make the best of it. At least it was quieter here, she thought, and she began cleaning a place on the couch to lie down.

She nodded off and was woken by Lucinda shaking her awake. It was fully dark now.

"Wake up. The justice officers are here. Someone

must have informed on you. You have to flee. Go through the window and along the roof. At the end of the building is a ladder, which will take you down to the street. Moons know what they will do to me if they find you here. Go!"

Lucinda's terrified expression was enough motivation, but she also heard men shouting, doors being broken open, and heavy footsteps on the stairs below.

She ran to the window, opened it, and scrambled down to the roof, cursing Farinelli for betraying her. Running along the peak of the roof she thanked the moons that it wasn't raining because the metal would have been very slippery otherwise. She ran about one hundred feet to the gable end, where she saw a ladder protruding from the wall. She climbed down the three stories as quickly as possible and jumped the remaining five feet into a dark alley. There were piles of garbage everywhere, but there was no sign of the Justice men. A sudden hiss caused her to scream and jump back, but it was just a wyvern feeding on some offal. She pulled her hood over her head and emerged into the street. All seemed normal.

CHAPTER 14

Millicent, realizing she was not far from her fencing tutor, went to him and asked for help.

She knocked on the door, and after a few moments, Benedict answered. His eyes were wide with surprise.

"It's me, Millicent, let me in."

"Millicent... Why are you here?"

"Just let me in, you oaf!" She pushed her way in and saw across the room a boy, a fencing student.

"Wait in there until my lesson is over." Benedict motioned to a side room where students dressed.

She heard the lesson commence and waited, helping herself to a cold pork pie she found on the table.

After an hour, she heard the student leave, and Benedict came to the room. "Now, why are you here and dressed so ridiculously? Did you eat my supper?"

"I need your help. My father was deposed, and now the Justice Ministry is trying to kill me; they killed my tutor, Nicodemus."

"What? By the moons!" He got up and began pacing, deep in thought.

"We'll have to get you out of the city."

"No, I can't. I have to rescue my father first. Can I hide here for a few days?"

"What? No. There is no room, and there are students coming and going."

"Where do you sleep?"

He scowled. "If they are looking for you, they might look here; it's not safe."

"Please, Benedict, I need help." This was the first time she had addressed him by his given name.

"Very well. I will find a place to hide you. Stay here; when I return, I will bring you to a nice, safe place."

In about an hour, he returned.

"I found a place for you to hide. It's not a palace, but you will be safe."

The streets were empty, which made her even more nervous. Their boot falls echoed in her ears like hammer blows. They walked about ten blocks to a nondescript building in the warehouse district.

He took out a key, unlocked the door, and motioned for her to enter. It was completely dark inside and stank of fish. The door closed behind her, and rough hands grabbed her. A lamp was lit, and she saw five justice officers surrounding her. Before she could even scream, they quickly stuffed a rag in her mouth and secured it with a chord, then tied her hands in front of her.

Benedict took a coin purse from one of the officers, glanced back at her, smirking, then left.

Muffled obscenities that would make a sailor blush were screamed through her gag.

One of the officers smiled and said, "We'll get a nice bonus for this."

Another said, "Why don't we have a little fun with her first."

The first one said, "No, we were ordered to bring her unharmed."

They dragged her out to the street; a carriage was coming, and she needed to act fast. She began making dramatic gagging sounds.

"What's she doing?"

"She's choking, I think."

"She's faking."

She pretended to faint.

"Better take the gag off; if she dies, we are in deep shit."

They took the gag off, and she coughed to clear her voice. Then, she croaked, "Zarblerg!"

With a pop, her demon appeared, and she shouted, "Kill them!"

"They didn't tell us she had a demon!"

"Doesn't look like much of a demon; we can take

it."

Zarblerg charged, making a ridiculous squeal, but it succeeded in forcing the guards to unhand her and draw their swords. As they fought, she ran, not looking back.

"After her!"

Footfalls followed her immediately, but she could tell it was just one guard, and with every block, she gained a bigger lead. She kept turning corners and then ducked into a dark alley, hoping she had lost him. Immediately, she began sawing at the rope binding her wrists against the sharp stone corner of the building. Too slow! She tried to reach her stiletto, but her bindings would not allow her to access that pocket. Footsteps were approaching. Looking around wildly for something to use as a weapon, she found a piece of wood on the ground that could be used as a club, and she could pick it up with her bound hands. She raised the club above her head to strike.

A man's head appeared, and she walloped him with the club. He fell like a sack of potatoes. The man was indeed the guard that was chasing her, and his sword was out, so she braced the sword between her legs and managed to cut the ropes binding her wrists in a few seconds. He began to stir and groan, so she grabbed his hair, tilted back his head, and cut the officer's neck with her stiletto, whispering to him, "This will teach you to kidnap young girls!"

"Zarblerg," she whispered. The demon appeared but was writhing on the ground; one of its legs was gone and had several other gashes.

"Moons! Are you alright?" she squealed.

"Yes, mistress, I killed one, but I need to go back to my plane to heal with your permission." It sounded clearly in distress.

"Yes, granted!"

Dashing between the shadows of the street lights, she returned to the crypt without incident, finally feeling safe in the tomb's darkness.

Climbing back down the ladder, she hoped she would be able to find her way back to Aldous, but she dared not summon Zarblerg, knowing he needed time to heal. After an hour or so, she had to admit she was lost.

"Aldous!" she yelled. Adramalech!" The tunnels stifled her shouts, and she felt claustrophobic. She sat down and tried to calm herself.

After a time, she heard the distant slithering of the powerful demon. She shivered, not relishing the thought of seeing the creature again.

Adramalech came into view and stopped. "Take me to Aldous," she commanded nervously.

Aldous somehow knew she was coming and exclaimed, "Millicent! I have found out some things since you've been gone. Your father is being held in the Justice Tower, as I suspected. Unfortunately, the tower has a powerful counter-spell that prevents any magic from being used within its walls, nor can any demon materialize or dematerialize inside the tower. We must find out where exactly in the tower he is before we can proceed."

"I know how we can do that."

She told Aldous all about her magic bird.

He agreed it was a good plan, but it was nighttime, and she was exhausted, so it would have to wait until morning.

Despite the hard pallet and thunderous snoring of Aldous, she was so tired that she fell asleep quickly.

CHAPTER 15

Millicent woke, but Aldous was still asleep, and she sensed that it was still nighttime. Not being able to go back to sleep, she summoned Zarblerg. He looked better. His wounds were closed, and he had a nub that was the beginnings of his leg growing back.

Thoughts of recent happenings rushed through her mind, and she began to fume.

"Benedict, that bastard betrayed me Zarblerg! I saw him pocket a sack of gold, no doubt in payment for giving me up. When this is over, I swear I will make him pay. I won't kill him; that's too good for him; just make him suffer for the rest of his life. He will be so miserable he will want to kill himself, but we won't let him." She babbled on for a time, brainstorming many creative and sadistic ways to torment him, and began to feel better.

"Will you help me with that, Zarblerg?"

"Yes, mistress, I would like that."

Aldous coughed and woke up.

"Oh, is that your demon?" he said in a tone of impressiveness.

"Yes, well, he fought for me and helped me to escape twice; he's not so bad. Is it daytime yet?"

CHAPTER 16

Millicent found an excellent place to conduct her crow reconnaissance: the top of the crypt. Sitting down in the center of the roof, she was invisible from the ground but had a large area from which to take off. Getting up was easy: climbing the vines clinging to the stonework.

With some trepidation, remembering the last experience, she took out the gonagas, closed her eyes, visualized the crow, and spoke the word of power. The transference of her soul to the figurine was as instantaneous but not quite as jarring as the first time. She took off and flew in the direction of the Justice Tower. The city looked splendid from the air. The smog wasn't so bad, and she had a clear view of the tower district. She flew so high the people on the ground looked like ants.

She planned to start at the top and circle the building, looking into each window for any sign of her father or prison cells. The tall but narrow windows afforded a good view into the tower's interior, and her bird eyes were sharp. Most of the top rooms were opulent offices used by the most important officials, but there were some storage rooms and other rooms whose purpose she could only guess.

After circling the building five times, she still had no glimpse of her father or prison cells, but she spotted something unusual on the sixth. There was a room filled with strange and elaborate tech devices that defied her powers of description, including a stout wooden chair with wires coming out of it. She landed on the window pane for a better look, but the instant her talons touched the stone, she returned to her body, and the crow figurine was gone. She was disoriented for a few moments, but it was much better than the first time, and she soon felt herself again.

CHAPTER 17

"The tower's anti-magic properties no doubt broke the spell that animated the crow. It probably turned back into a statue the moment it was in range, sending your spirit back into your body," Aldous said.

"And now my crow is gone, and we still don't know where my father is."

"Don't worry; I think we can assume he is on one of the top floors of the tower. I have a plan." He smiled, pleased with himself.

She held up her hands in exasperation. "Are you going to tell me?"

"Yes, that was a dramatic pause. I have sent Adramalech back to his plane. There, he will kill and consume demons with the power of flight, this will cause him to gain such power. Then, we will fly to the tower, rescue him, and fly back."

"Won't the anti-magic stop Adramalech from getting in?"

"No, demons are not magical in the same sense as the crow was. Demons cannot materialize or dematerialize inside the tower but can certainly walk or fly inside if they are already in this plane."

"How long will it take?"

"No idea. I should think about a few days at least."

The thought of spending a few days in these dank tunnels nauseated her, so she devised a plan to get her crow back.

She made her way back to the crypt entrance, this time marking the way with some soft rock she had found on the ground. There, she summoned Zarblerg.

His wounds had healed, and his nub of a leg was more prominent, although still too short for him to walk on.

"Say, Zar. If you killed some flying demons, could you gain the power of flight?"

"Apologies, mistress, I am not powerful enough to kill a flying demon."

"Oh, pity. Well, maybe someday. Go back and heal up now. Stammi bene."

It was still daytime, so she waited on the crypt roof until dark, watching the clouds roll by.

Millicent walked the streets, dressed again as a boy, ducking into dark alleys whenever she saw anything that warned her of a justice officer. In one of these alleys, she found a ramshackle structure made of discarded wood. She peered inside. There were three small children, filthy and in rags. The oldest, a boy, picked up a stick and snarled at her like a dog.

Millicent bent down and said gently, "Don't worry, I'm not going to hurt you. I want to pay you to do me a little favor."

The boy didn't respond and kept the stick up defensively.

"Look," she said, taking a shiny coin from her purse.

His eyes lit up, and she gave him the instructions. She told him where the justice tower was and which side of the building to look at. She only hoped that the crow figurine had fallen into the bushes surrounding the building and was not taken by someone. He ran off, and impatiently, she waited.

Hours passed, and she began to think that the urchin had taken it to a pawnbroker and sold it himself for more money. She began to get angry. Just then, she heard small bare feet approaching, and the boy appeared. He grinned and pulled out the figurine. Or was it a grimace?

Then, a strange mechanical clanking could be heard approaching. Millicent looked around, but there was no escape; she was trapped. She took out her stiletto. The boy dashed into his hovel.

In the alley appeared two half-human, half-clockwork monsters; homunculi. She heard rumors of the new creatures designed by the Tech Ministry to be used as justice officers but had yet to see one. They had human faces, although their skin was pallid and gray, like a dead creature, and a glass eyepiece was attached to one eye. One of their arms was made of metal and gears, and one had two clockwork legs. They carried only a club on their belt, and their hands held no weapon. She was trained well, but facing off against two large men armed with only a knife was not good odds.

Stifling a scream, she called for Zarblerg instead. He appeared but immediately fell over, having only one leg, and began squealing fiercely at the attackers. The homunculi ignored him and came at her. They were utterly fearless, indeed, seemed without any emotion. Before they could grab her arm, she cut one's throat, which should have been fatal, but the monster did not so much as bleed. It was then she noticed the creature's face; it was the one that followed her into the alley, the one whose throat she cut, she was sure. These creatures were made from the dead!

They backed her against the wall and grabbed her.

With incredible efficiency, she was trussed up with a cord and made wholly incapacitated. They carried her off to the main road, Zarblerg squealing most pitifully but could not follow. They stood there in the street and waited for something while she was trussed up, helpless like a pig. Citizens passing by stared at her. She felt humiliated and furious but could not move a muscle or scream.

A Justice carriage appeared, and she was thrown in. On the floor and not being able to move, she had difficulty seeing but ended up where she guessed was the justice tower. They carried her up countless floors, and she found herself in a tiny cell with no furniture. Two human justice officers untied her, took her belongings, and handed her a dry set of clothing.

"If you think I am changing into this drab sack cloth, you are crazy!"

The guards left and returned a moment later with a bucket of water, which they threw on her.

The outfit was coarse prisoner fare and much too big for her, but she was cold and reluctantly changed into dry clothing. Mercifully, they left her alone so she had privacy. She tried summoning Zarblerg, but as expected, nothing happened. She tried a spell to light up the room as an experiment, but it also failed. Her magic was gone entirely. The guards soon returned and took her old clothes and belongings.

CHAPTER 18

When Zarblerg was summoned and saw its mistress being attacked, it was angry and wanted to destroy the creatures but could only crawl very slowly because it only had one leg. The only thing it could do was kill and eat the boy human that brought the bad people to its mistress. Not knowing what else to do, Zarblerg returned to its plane to heal. As it healed, it thought deeply about what to do but found it very difficult, the world of humans being a complete mystery to it. Another demon that passed by berated it and advised it to return to the human plane and consume more humans to learn more about their world. This is what Zarblerg resolved to do.

CHAPTER 19

After a few hours, Millicent's cell door opened, and Director Aldebrand stepped in.

Aldebrand, "Do you remember me?"

"How could I forget that ugly face?" she said defiantly, refusing to show any fear.

"You almost killed me, you know. Tell me, was it for a demon-summoning ritual?" His tone was nonchalant, almost conversational.

"Yes, but the demon that came was pitiful; now I see why."

"Indeed, as I was still alive. But that is not why you are here. Do you know why you are here?"

She glared at him defiantly.

"Well, I will tell you. For some time now, the Magic Ministry led by your father has been practicing illegal magic. Furthermore, he has been interfering with the Tech Ministry and the wonderful inventions they have given us."

"What are you talking about, you idiot? My father would never practice illegal magic."

"Ah, but he did."

"Chissenefrega! Is he alive?"

"Yes, he will stand trial."

"My aunt?"

"She died while being arrested. Unfortunate. The officers responsible have been disciplined. But now we have you, so all is well."

Without warning, she attacked, striking with her fist for his larynx, but Aldebrand was strong and quick and held her off. She relaxed and made him think she had given up while he held her arms but kicked for his balls. He cried in pain but held on and slammed her against the wall, stunning her.

"You'll pay for that, you little witch. Guards! Time to see your father."

Two officers returned and manacled her wrists, leading her away, Aldebrand in the lead. They said nothing, not responding to her curses. Going up one more set of stairs, they came to a room labeled "Office of Inquiries." When the door opened, it looked like the one she spotted as a crow before she landed on the ledge, and the spell was broken.

Inside the room was her father. She gasped; his appearance shocked her. He was sitting on a stout wooden chair with a cacophony of wires, metal tubes, and gadgets attached to it. Two pieces of metal were attached to his head near the temples. His clothing was torn and soiled, and he looked dazed.

Three other men were in the room. Morcant, the Justice Minister, was a tall man of middle age, bald, with a thick mustache, and heavily muscled. Tranton, the Tech Minister, was an older, tall, gaunt man with an enormous hawk nose and deep set eyes that were too close together. Finally, there was a technician dressed in overalls named Cynebald.

Morcant, "Lucian, look who is here to see you."

Slowly, he looked up and grimaced. Millicent was shocked. It was the first time she had ever seen him look afraid.

Morcant, "Now, be a good fellow and tell us what we need to know, and we can release you both."

"We both know you will never release us," Lucian said, his voice full of defeat.

"Yes, you pose too much of a risk, but your young daughter is no threat to us. Now let's be reasonable," Morcant said.

His head hung back down.

"Very well. Take him down."

Cynebald released him from the chair, and the two guards dragged him to the corner of the room. He was limp and had to be almost carried.

"Now her."

Aldebrand grabbed Millicent and thrust her into the chair. She resisted, but he was solid, and with the help of Cynebald, she was restrained.

Tranton began to speak, "You see, Millicent. Your

father withholds certain information which is very important to the Tech Ministry. Some years ago, a miraculous discovery was made, an incredible new source of power called electricity. But despite our best efforts, any attempt to harness this force inside the city failed. Then, by accident, we discovered that electricity works inside the Justice Tower within the range of our spell-canceling equipment and so deduced that a spell was in force, which somehow dampens the use of electricity inside the city. Since the Ministry of Magic had been arguing against using electricity from the beginning, the source of the spell was obvious.

"Your electricity counteracts magic. If you get what you want, magic will be gone, and our way of life will be destroyed," Lucian said.

"That is yet to be proven, but even so, technology is the way of the future. If magic is displaced, it is a worthy price for the good of Rathberg," answered Tranton.

"Let's show them the power of which we speak, Minister," Morcant said to Tranton.

Tranton nodded at Cynebald, and he pulled a lever.

Lucian screamed in rage.

Instantly, Millicent felt like she was on fire. Her eyesight was lost in a white flash, and her body convulsed as if every muscle in her body fired off at once. After an endless moment, the lever was lifted, and the pain was mostly gone. She could smell her hair burning, and she felt weak, could barely move, and had trouble thinking.

"Does that loosen your tongue, former director?" Morcant said. "Very well..."

"Stop!" Lucian yelled, his tone and body language defeated. "You must promise to not harm my daughter."

"You are in no position to negotiate-" Tranton started.

Morcant held up his hand. "Your daughter is no threat to us. We agree to your terms. She will not be harmed."

"There is a crystal hidden at the top of the Clockwork Spire. Destroy the crystal and the galvanic-dampening spell will be broken," said Lucian.

"There, now, so much unpleasantness could have been avoided," Tranton said.

They dragged out Millicent's limp body.

Tranton whispered something to one of the guards, who quickly left.

"We will wait to confirm what you said is true," Tranton said to Lucian.

"I give you my word," Lucian croaked.

"I believe you, but it is the scientific way to confirm everything with data."

CHAPTER 20

Some time passed, during which Millicent began to recover from her ordeal.

The guard returned and whispered to Morcant.

"Excellent, the crystal has been found and destroyed," Morcant said.

"Put him back in the chair," Tranton said to Cynebald.

"He told you what you wanted; let him go!" Millicent shouted.

"Gag her," ordered Aldebrand.

She bit one of the guards, almost severing his finger, but the other one slapped her so hard she briefly lost consciousness, and they put on the gag.

Morcant turned to Tranton, approached him, and whispered something to him. They had a brief whispered conversation, after which Morcant seemed appeased.

"Do as I commanded," Tranton said.

They strapped Lucian back into the chair.

"You can help us in one final way, former

Minister. Technician, turn it up to maximum, and let's observe the results," Tranton said.

Cynebald pulled the lever, and sparks emitted from the plates by her father's temples. His entire body convulsed so strongly that the chair rocked. The lever remained down, and seconds passed until Lucian's hair caught fire.

Millicent screamed.

"Stop. Now take his pulse," Tranton ordered.

Cynebald did so and shook his head.

"Good. Be sure to keep careful notes on the experiment, including voltage and elapsed time," said Tranton.

Millicent was numb with grief, she felt like she was in a nightmare.

"Take her away," said Morcant.

"Don't worry, I will keep my promise; you will not be harmed," Morcant told Millicent as they dragged her away.

Out of the corner of her eye, she saw movement outside the window. She turned and was amazed to see Aldous atop a flying demon. Like a caterpillar transforming into a moth, Adramalech now had wings and a much thinner body. With an enormous crash, the demon broke the window and squeezed in through the tall, narrow opening. Everyone inside was momentarily stunned, but Millicent heard Aldous shout, "Millicent, jump on!" she dashed past the stunned guards and jumped on the demon's back. Quickly, the demon spun and launched out the window, but not before one of the guards slashed the creatures back, missing Millicent by inches. It struggled with the girl's additional weight and could barely keep aloft. Then she saw its wing was severely damaged by the sword, and a green ichor that was its blood was spraying out. She heard Aldous shout, "Oh dear." Then they plummeted. They fell some 150 feet, and Millicent blacked out.

CHAPTER 21

Millicent was fortunate that Aldous fell off the demon before they hit the ground, allowing it to at least slow its descent due to its reduced weight. When they landed, Adramalech was below her, and despite being crushed into an unrecognizable jelly, its great bulk dampened a great deal of the fall for her, saving her life.

An indeterminate time later, she woke in a bed in enormous pain. She could see that her legs were bound in splints. There was a moment of panic when she realized she couldn't move her arms, but then turned to see her wrists were in restraints. She considered plans of escape. She tried to call for Zarblerg, but he could or would not come. Two guards were posted at her door, and the window was too small for her to fit through, even if she could escape from her restraints. A nurse came and forced a potion down her throat. She slept.

Aldebrand's face appeared, hovering over her, and he said quietly and calmly, "You are a fortunate girl, surviving a fall of over 150 feet. Morcant is determined to keep his promise and ensure you are not harmed, although I made a great effort to impress upon him how dangerous a little witch like you can be. I have the scars to attest to that. However, you may wish you had died in the fall when you recover and are sent to Bedlam; I have that to console me at least."

"Mollami," was all she could muster in response before she passed out again from the pain.

Days, then weeks, passed in a haze caused by the pain potions given to her. When conscious, her thoughts turned to brainstorming and planning ever more diabolical revenge on her enemies. A raven never forgets who wronged them, she kept telling herself.

One day, her casts were removed. Every day, nurses made her endure the agony of walking on her newly healed legs. They meant well, and she cooperated and improved quickly. After a few more weeks, with the help of some powerful healing magic, she could almost walk as normal.

Then, one day, two guards came in and trussed her up, and gagged her. She fought mightily until a burly nurse came in and forced a potion down her throat, which made her fall asleep.

They loaded her into a coach and took her to another part of the city, to her new home, the Bedlam Reform Institution.

CHAPTER 22

The Bedlam Reform Institution was a large rectangular building on the outskirts of the city. Like the Tower of Justice, it had magic-dampening tech in effect. Millicent could feel the low hum of a machine droning somewhere in the facility. It seemed to penetrate her skull and give her a constant headache. She tried all manner of spells, but none had any effect whatsoever.

For the first few days, Millicent behaved well, observing everything carefully, making mental notes of all the security features, escape always at the back of her mind. All the inmates (or patients as the nurses called them) were issued drab, loose-fitting, gray clothing. She had her own tiny cell with nothing but a small, hard bed and a thin blanket. At night, they were all locked in their cells, but they were allowed to go from the bedroom ward to a large common area during the day. The inmates were all female, as were most of the staff. Only the guards were male but were required to wear faceless white masks while on duty. The inmates were mainly her age or a little older; none were over twenty. Some were quite evidently insane, but most appeared ordinary, at least most of the time. At night, there was often screaming and sounds of hysteria from the other cells. The thought of escape never left her mind, and she brainstormed and plotted, constantly running escape plans through her mind.

A week after she had been admitted, she was eating in the common room and overheard a few girls from another table talking about her. They kept glancing at her and saying things like "posh girl," "they say she is the daughter of a minister," and "never had to lift a finger in her life"...

Millicent kept her cool but didn't forget. Later in the week, a girl named Sabina, the leader of the gang and a little older but much bigger, was walking in the hallway and deliberately walked into her so hard that she fell, causing the group to laugh.

"Watch where you're walking, Minister's daughter. People aren't going to make way for you here," said Sabina.

Millicent popped right up and said, "Say you're sorry."

They laughed.

The girl was tall, so Millicent could barely reach her head, so she punched her in the gut, in a place that she learned would make the person double over and gasp for breath, then grabbed her hair and kneed her in the face, breaking her nose.

The guards sprang into action and grabbed Millicent, one guard holding each arm, and they dragged her away to her cell and locked her in.

She was locked in her cell for a week, and the guards brought her food twice a day. At the end of the week, the cell door opened, and the administrator entered. The administrator was a tall, middle-aged woman with a stern countenance and severe, almost masculine clothing.

"The penalty for your first offense is a week of confinement in your room. The second offense will be a month."

"And the third offense?" Millicent defiantly asked.

"Have you seen the girl who sits by the window but never speaks? She has a scar on her head. You could ask her, although she can no longer speak, so she wouldn't answer."

Millicent stayed away from the cruel girls and stayed out of trouble, and a few more weeks passed.

CHAPTER 23

In the meantime, Sabina was plotting revenge. She managed to bribe a guard to smuggle in a particular potion made from a fungus. During mealtime, the girls created a distraction that caused Millicent to turn her head, during which one of the girls poured the potion into her porridge. After her meal, Millicent caught Sabina glaring at her, then looked away quickly when she saw Millicent was watching. At the time, she thought nothing of it.

About an hour later, with no warning, Millicent felt like her spirit had left her body, and she was watching the world from afar or through a fog. Her senses were intact, but everything seemed unreal, as if she were in a dream or nightmare. It was as if she were one of those homunculus creatures and controlled a machine that was not her own body. Terrified, she ran to her room, cowering there for the day and a night and a half the next day, hoping that her symptoms would subside and she would feel herself again. Finally, hunger and thirst overtook her, and she went to the common room to eat. She did not engage with anyone and barely even noticed anyone else. Those watching her would see her considerably changed, with the spark extinguished from her eyes, a downcast expression, and a slow, robotic manner of moving.

Finally, that night, Millicent was able to sleep. When she woke, she felt only marginally better; perhaps she was only getting used to her condition. First, she blamed her symptoms on being locked up in prison and her father being murdered, the trauma finally overtaking her, but then she remembered how Sabina looked at her and became suspicious, theorizing that she had been poisoned.

Every night, she prayed to the moons for her condition to improve, but months passed, and they did not. Finally, she resigned herself to her condition and became determined to resume her plans for escape and revenge.

CHAPTER 24

When Zarblerg was fully healed, it returned to the human plane and tried to materialize near its mistress, but something was blocking it. She was being kept in some building with barred windows and could only materialize outside some outer walls, which were warded against demons and prevented him from scaling or penetrating. So, without a plan, the demon returned to the streets of the harlot district and observed, remaining invisible, endeavoring to learn more about the human plane. Occasionally, it would kill and consume a human that seemed intelligent, and slowly, it learned. Also, occasionally, it would return to where its mistress was imprisoned and try to find her. After a dozen or so victims, Zarblerg began to understand humans and remembered when its mistress told him about the one called Benedict. He had betrayed her, and she had made Zarblerg promise to torture him but not kill him, this he resolved to do.

It took many more victims, but finally, he consumed one with the knowledge of where this Benedict was and paid him a visit, observing invisibly for many days. The demon deduced that this human function was to train young humans how to fight. During a sword fighting lesson with a boy, Zarblerg grabbed Benedict's hand and forced him to strike the boy dead, remaining invisible the whole time. Zarblerg could smell the fear and anguish coming from Benedict and knew what he did would please his mistress. Zarblerg watched as the human dragged the corpse out to an alley and left it there. The next day, a man came asking for the boy, but Benedict told him a lie.

Zarblerg settled into a pattern of keeping vigil at the prison of its mistress, watching and tormenting Benedict, and killing humans.

One day, while keeping vigil at the Bedlam Institution, Zarblerg realized that if it materialized up a tree by the walls, it could see over the wall and into the building. This it did and soon saw its mistress inside through some windows; she was sitting at a table. Zarblerg learned that she would be there often during the day, so it patiently sat vigil up the tree daily.

CHAPTER 25

Millicent was staring out the window, which was now her favorite pastime, and thought she could see someone or something watching from up a tree. She blinked, not daring to believe, thinking she might be hallucinating. She squinted; yes, it was Zarblerg; she was almost sure. One of the girls wore spectacles, and Millicent gently took them from her, thinking she would not react since she was mostly catatonic and seldom moved and had to be led to and from her room by the staff, but the instant her glasses were removed the girl began screeching in such a loud and strident tone that everyone in the room turned to look. The guards came and, knowing what happened, grabbed her and took away the spectacles, but not before she put them on and got a good look outside. It was definitely Zarblerg.

This was her second offense, and she was confined to her cell, this time for a month. Her tiny cell window faced the other direction from where her demon was, but she was nevertheless encouraged that it was faithful and could perhaps assist her escape, at least once she got past the walls. She tried to think of ways to get him a message.

Millicent sat in the common room, listening to one of the patients playing the accordion (she was terrible). There was a commotion from the hallway where the bedrooms were. A couple of guards entered a room while two others guarded the door. After a few moments, the administrator entered and left with the guards a few minutes later. Then, two nurses entered with a rolling cart. After a time, they left, and only one guard remained, his back to the door. She could hear some of the girls chattering and gathered that one of the girls had hung herself in her room; it was something that happened not infrequently. After about another hour, two guards arrived with a gurney, entered the room, and then left with the girl's body wrapped from head to toe in her white sheets. She watched from the window as the body wagon exited the gates with the corpse. Millicent had the beginnings of a plan.

CHAPTER 26

Patiently, Zarblerg watched Benedict, causing him misfortune whenever the demon saw an opportunity. The demon often tripped him, pushed him, caused objects to fall on him, and fouled his food. Occasionally, the demon would go out to kill and consume more humans for sport and to learn more about this strange new world.

One night, Benedict went to a place of gambling and threw cubic objects with numbers onto a table. Zarblerg was confused, so it killed a man who was leaving the place and learned about dice. With this knowledge it made Benedict lose every time by invisibly turning the dice to the bad numbers. His anguish was most gratifying.

Another night Benedict went to a whorehouse and paid a woman to mate with him. Zarblerg strangled her as they fornicated, and Benedict was forced to escape out the window and run home without clothing on.

One day, Benedict went to an influential man's house and met alone with him in a room. Zarblerg opened a tiny portal to his plane, filling the room with a smell that humans hated. The important man became angry, and Benedict was ordered to leave. His suffering was delicious, and it made the demon crave more. The following night, Benedict went to a place where men drink, and he kept pushing his cup off the table, forcing the man to buy another cup. Then, he threw the drink into the face of another man nearby. This man attacked Benedict, and they fought; other men joined in, and the mayhem pleased Zarblerg. Benedict staggered out of the place badly beaten and crawled into an alley, barely able to move.

"By the moon, why is this misfortune happening to me!" he cried.

After a time, he was able to stagger home. After drinking an entire bottle of brandy, he tied a rope around a beam in the ceiling, got on a chair and tied the other end around his neck, and jumped. Zarblerg knew this would kill him, and that was not allowed by his mistress' instructions, so he caused the rope to break.

Benedict sobbed bitterly, not rising from the floor. "I know you are a demon; why do you torment me?! Show yourself!"

Zarblerg was obedient by nature and could think of no reason to stay hidden so materialized.

Benedict's eyes widened in horror. "Who are you? Who sent you?"

"My mistress Millicent sent me."

"Millicent! Of course! That bitch!"

This angered Zarblerg, and the demon kicked Benedict in the head.

After a time, Benedict said softly, "Where is she?"

"She is inside a building surrounded by a wall I am not allowed to pass."

"Is the building rectangular shaped, one story, and surrounded by a brick wall," asked Benedict.

"Yes," answered Zarblerg.

"Yes, it must be the Bedlam Institute," Benedict said.

He sat for a time, then had an idea, "Will you stop tormenting me if I help Millicent escape from that place?"

Zarblerg considered for several moments and finally decided it was a good bargain, "Yes, you will help my mistress escape."

CHAPTER 27

Benedict was cunning, and with the promise of his lousy luck being lifted, he put great effort into the plan to rescue Millicent. His first point of action was to get her a message, but this would be challenging because ordinary citizens were not allowed into the institute, and it did not allow visitors.

"Demon," Benedict said gingerly, not enjoying its presence.

It materialized, and he continued, "I need money to bribe a guard to help Millicent escape. I need your help to make me money."

"How?"

"We will go back to the gambling hall, and this time, you will help me win."

They returned, and Benedict bet the meager remainder of his savings and kept winning. He was enjoying himself, but from the looks of people, he knew they were beginning to suspect he was cheating, so he stopped, gathered his earnings, and left. As he left the building, he glanced back and noticed some roughs had followed him.

"Demon, the men behind me mean to steal this money. Can you stop them?"

He hurried along, hoping the demon had heard and would help. The men behind him quickened their pace and gained on him. He spun around and drew his sword. It was three men, and each had a cudgel. He could fight off two men with a sword, but three was dangerous even for an expert swordsman like himself. When they were just a few feet away, Zarblerg materialized and quickly bit one of the men's faces off. The others ran away.

"I like having you on my side," Benedict said as he sheathed his sword.

CHAPTER 28

Benedict leaned casually against a wall with a view to the gates of the Bedlam Asylum and waited. He noted when the shifts changed and ordered Zarblerg to follow one of the guards he picked out and report back on everything he did.

This first guard was a simple man who did nothing but work, eat, and care for his elderly mother. He did not seem to be in great need of money, so he was unsuitable.

The next man the demon followed was more promising. He was a family man but spent most nights drinking, gambling, and cheating on his wife. Benedict began following him, keeping up the surveillance for a week, watching him while he drank in his tavern while Zarblerg observed invisibly.

"Demon, I think this is our man. But we have to put the pressure on him. Watch him and be sure that he loses when he gambles. We need him to be desperate."

A week passed, and Benedict decided it was time to approach the guard. While he walked home from the tavern late one night, Benedict lay in wait and knocked him out with a club when he passed a dark alley. The man, named Donal, woke up tied to a chair in an abandoned warehouse—the very one, in fact, that Millicent was lured to. His eyes cleared, and he saw Benedict in front of him. Then he saw the demon standing next to Benedict and screamed.

"What's happening? What have I done?"

"You have gambled away your savings and left your wife and children in a dire condition. And I am here to help you."

"Help me? How? What the hell is that hideous thing?" exclaimed Donal.

"I'm not sure what to call it, but I've seen it bite a man's face clean off, so I wouldn't insult it like that. Now, here is what's going to happen. I will pay you 100 ducats a week, and in exchange, you will do me some small favors."

"What favors?" Donal said suspiciously.

"Take a message with you into the institution, give it to a girl named Millicent, and bring back to me her reply, that is all."

"If I get caught, they will put me in prison."

"So don't get caught, or would you rather your children be orphaned?" Benedict threatened.

He grimaced, looking like a trapped animal, then finally said, "Yeah, alright, I can do it."

"I will be in your local tavern tomorrow night.

And if you try to betray me, I will know, and I will let my friend here do terrible things to you. He will be watching you," Benedict turned to the demon, "Become invisible, go behind the man, and box his ears."

The demon obeyed, and Donal screamed when his ears were invisibly boxed, "Alright! I understand. I will not betray you."

"Good," Benedict untied him, handed him a note folded up very small, and left.

CHAPTER 29

The following morning, Millicent found a tiny piece of paper in her room that had been stuffed through the peephole during the night.

It read, "Millicent. Your demon and I are vigilantly planning your escape. We have bribed one of the guards to relay messages to us. Destroy this message after you read it and leave your reply inside page 10 of a book you leave on your bed; the guard will take it when no one is looking. Yours, B."

She was all at once both overjoyed and confused. Who was B? She thought hard. The only person she knew with that initial was Benedict and he betrayed her. Was this another trick? Perhaps Zarblerg convinced him to help, but she didn't think the demon was bright enough. Nevertheless, she had to take the chance. She tore up the note, threw it down the sewer pipe, ripped off a small piece of paper from one of her books, and began furiously writing.

"Benedict, you miserable cocksucker, if this is a trick-"

She stopped. If he were really trying to help her, she should be nice. She destroyed her note and started again.

"B. I am grateful for your help. I can see my demon when he watches me from over the wall. So that I can be sure it is you, and you intend to help me, have him hold one hand in the air so I can be sure you are really working together."

She folded the note and put it inside the book as instructed. When the doors were unlocked, she went to the common room and tried to see if any of the guards seemed different, but they did not. Knowing she now had allies, she eagerly plotted her escape.

The following day, there was no note, but she wasn't concerned. Instead, she watched for Zarblerg to wave. At the usual time, he appeared, as always, and then he held his arm up awkwardly.

She grinned and returned to her room to write another note.

"I have a plan. In a week, on the morning of the half and quarter moons, the body wagon will leave the hospital an hour or so before midday with one corpse. I will be the corpse. It is vital that our guard be the one guarding the room with the dead body. Don't fail me!"

CHAPTER 30

Benedict sat with Donal in the pub and read the note. His eyebrows arched, and he smiled a little.

"In a week, on the morning of the half and quarter moons, there will be a death. You must be the one guarding the body," Benedict said to Donal.

"What? I thought I was only to smuggle some notes?"

"Listen, you degenerate gambler," Benedict leaned close over the table. If you don't do this, it will not end well for you." Then, in a kinder tone, he added, "If you do well, however, this will be the last thing I ask of you. Now, will you do it, or do I have to summon my demon?"

"Yes, very well," he said, grimacing like a man that was just condemned.

CHAPTER 31

The night before the half and quarter moons, Millicent enacted her plan. In the middle of the night, she rose from her bed and used a lock pick she fashioned out of two forks to unlock her door. From an early age, she was fascinated by locks and taught herself the art of picking, stubbornly sticking with it, practicing on any lock she could find, and eventually becoming adept.

The hallway was deserted, and the institution was as quiet as a crypt. Millicent went to Sabina's door, picked the lock, and entered as quietly as she could, standing silently for a moment to ensure Sabina was still asleep. Then she took a scarf from her pocket and crept to the bed. Gripping the ends of the scarf with both hands, she quickly slipped it underneath Sabina's neck and tightened it with all her strength. Sabina woke and struggled mightily. It took all of Millicent's strength to hold on as she was tossed about. After about 30 seconds, the girl stopped struggling, but Millicent kept the pressure around her neck for another minute to make sure she was dead and not just unconscious. She listened to make sure no one had heard the commotion and would come to investigate.

Next, she tore strips out of the bed sheets and fashioned a noose. She put the noose around Sabina's neck and wrapped the other end around a gas lamp projecting from the wall. She had to pull with all her strength and weight to raise the corpse off the ground and tie off the rope. Then she placed the wooden chair underneath and tipped it over to make it look like it was kicked out from underneath her.

With the grisly work done, she returned to her room, her excitement not allowing her to sleep.

In the morning, when the doors were being opened, she heard the commotion outside, indicating the body was found. Just as last time, the door was guarded while the other girls congregated in the main hall. When no one was looking, she went to the door, watching for any reaction from the guard. He completely ignored her as she entered Sabina's room. Sabina's corpse was there wrapped in white linen. Millicent busied herself with unwrapping the corpse, then stuffed the corpse under the bed, laid down where the corpse was, and began wrapping herself with the linen. It was tough when she got to her chest; she had to keep one arm free and wrap her body and head with one arm. The procedure was taking too long, and she feared she would run out of time and be discovered.

She heard activity from outside. The men with the gurney were coming. In the nick of time, she completed her wrapping.

She felt herself lifted and placed on the gurney, then felt the gurney being moved.

"Wait." She heard the voice of the administrator.

Panic rose in her breast; she was trapped, wrapped up like a bug in a web.

The administrator produced a long needle and poked the corpse in the arm. Millicent made no sound but could not help but twitch with the pain.

"She is alive, unwrap her."

The administrator scowled at Millicent, furious.

"Where is Sabina?"

After being that close to freedom, being caught was so devastating that she was close to tears and could not speak.

"Search the room," she told the guards.

"She is under the bed," said one of the guards.

"Did you kill her?"

"No! I just swapped places with her when I heard what happened!" Millicent pleaded.

"If you had killed her, the punishment would be the gallows, despite my promise to Minister Morcant to not harm you. Still, you will be severely punished for this."

"Confine her to her room and stand guard," she said to the guard as they left the room.

In the meantime, Benedict, wearing a black hood,

had ambushed the corpse wagon when it reached the morgue. At sword point, he made the drivers lay down on the ground while he tied them up. Then, he began unwrapping the corpse. To his alarm, the body was cold and clearly dead. He unwrapped the head and saw it was not Millicent. He cursed and ran off, narrowly escaping the justice officers who arrived at the scene.

Donal, who was off duty and sleeping in his bed by then, was arrested by a squad of justice officers who brought them to the Justice Tower Office of Inquiries. It was only a short time until he confessed everything and told the officers about the man who was paying him and the plan to free Millicent. He was forced to return with some undercover officers to the tavern where he was to meet Benedict, who wisely did not show up. At the same time, some officers came to the warehouse where Benedict first questioned Donal, but it was empty. Fortunately, they only had a rough description of Benedict, so they could not discover his identity.

A few hours later, her door opened, and the administrator entered with two guards. "Normally, the punishment for a third serious offense is an operation to the brain, which makes the subject completely compliant. But it has the unfortunate side effect of rendering the subject unable to speak or do much of anything for that matter. Luckily for you, the Tech Ministry has invented a new treatment. It is quite experimental but has shown good results with fewer side effects. Take her."

The guards took her roughly by the arms and dragged her off. They came through two locked doors to a stairway leading down. Through another hallway, she was led into a room. Inside was the same chair contraption as the Room of Inquiries, where her father was tortured. Standing by the chair was a technician dressed in white overalls. Upon seeing the device, she struggled and tried to escape, but the guards held on tightly. They bound her to the chair with leather straps, and the administrator and the two guards stood by as the technician prepared the equipment.

Helpless, Millicent knew what would come next and was powerless to stop it.

"No, please," she begged.

The lever was pulled, and she felt the violent white pain. After a brief pause, the lever was pulled again two more times, but by then, Millicent was unconscious.

Millicent woke up in her bed feeling extremely groggy. Her arms and legs felt like they were made of lead. She felt lightheaded and unmotivated, and despite not having eaten all day, she was not hungry.

The administrator entered, and she looked pleased. "How do you feel, Millicent?"

She wanted to curse at her but could not speak and could only stare with glazed eyes.

"Can you get up? It's been a whole day," she said in

a kindly tone.

Millicent did not move.

"No? Perhaps we need to use a little less power next time. Let's get some food into you, and you'll feel better."

A chair with wheels was rolled in, and two guards lifted her on and wheeled her to the common room. She was given a tray of food, and the administrator began feeding her like a baby, and she seemed to be enjoying herself.

After a few days, Millicent started to feel more like herself again. She did not see the guard, who was her ally, and greatly feared that he had been arrested. She wondered if Benedict had been caught and arrested.

The administrator came to her bed just after lockup. "You have caused quite the scandal here. The guard who was helping you will not return; in fact, his life is forfeit, and he has you to thank for it. Who was helping you from the outside?"

Millicent looked at her with hate-filled eyes.

"Come now, a man was seen attacking the corpse wagon on the morning of your adventure, but he got away."

A long, silent pause.

"Very well, I see you need more treatments. They will commence in the morning," she said sternly.

Millicent was terrified at the prospect of more

treatments and spent a sleepless night trying to brainstorm another way to escape.

In the morning, a guard took her to the basement. The technician was there, but not the administrator.

"Where is the administrator? I need her to be present for the interrogation," he said to the guard, who left, leaving just Millicent, who was restrained in the chair, and the technician.

Millicent saw an opportunity. "This technology is fascinating. How does it work."

He stared at her, shocked, as if unused to one of his lab rats speaking to him, but he quickly warmed.

"It is called electricity. It is a new form of power discovered by the Tech Ministry."

"Like a kind of magic?" She tried to sound like a dumb girl and smiled as charmingly as she could in the circumstances.

"No, electricity and magic seem to counteract each other. The magic dampening system for the institute works with electricity."

"Magic dampening?"

"Yes, a machine in the room next door prevents all magic from being focused in the building and its grounds, and it also prohibits demons and magical creatures from materializing."

Her pulse quickened, one machine, and she now knew where it was. She would be free if she could find a way to disable it.

The door opened, and the administrator entered; it was time for the treatment to begin.

She whimpered as they tied her down, but she refused to scream or beg.

Millicent awakened in her bed. She felt a little better than last time; in fact, she was cheerful because she had a plan.

Millicent knew she needed to feign compliance to gain their trust. When the administrator entered, she forced herself to smile sweetly.

"Well, you look much better today; I think the treatments are working."

"Yes, Administrator, I feel much better."

"Now, Millicent, will you tell me who your accomplice was?" the administrator said sternly.

"I'm sorry, I truly don't remember," Millicent said meekly.

"Well, memory loss is a side effect of the treatment we are beginning to learn. But don't fret; the important thing is you are becoming more agreeable."

"I would like to go to the common room now, please."

"Excellent!"

She was wheeled to the common room, and the administrator again fed her a spoonful at a time like a baby.

Afterward, Millicent asked, "Will I need more treatments, Administrator?"

She seemed to consider it and then said, "Oh yes, I think after a few more years, you will be completely rehabilitated."

Millicent thanked her as sweetly as she could manage, but in heart throbbed a black hatred she could barely contain.

CHAPTER 32

After a few days, when it was time for her subsequent treatment, she appeared so willing to the guard that he let her walk without restraining her. She paid close attention to the rooms and located the door where she thought the magic dampening equipment was.

Before she was strapped into the machine, she said, "Oh. Please, I need to pee!"

The technician looked dubious and glanced at the guard, who shook his head.

"I don't want to ruin your fine equipment," Millicent added.

"She is right; water is very bad for electric equipment," the technician told the guard.

"I will fetch a chamber pot," the guard said, then left the room.

Millicent smiled sweetly at the technician, and with all the charm she could muster, she said, "Your machine is very fine. What does that do?"

He turned slightly for a moment, and she burst into action, taking out a small knife she stole from the cafeteria, which she had sharpened carefully and hid in her clothing, and attacking the technician, severing his jugular expertly. She ran to the door which held the dampening equipment. It was locked – no time to pick the lock. Desperate, knowing she had only seconds before the guard would return, she ran to the technician and searched him, finding a set of keys in his pocket. The first key did not fit the lock. She tried the second. This one worked, and she was inside.

The room was a chaotic mess of wires, metal panels, gears, and all tech do-dads.

She heard shouting from outside; she would be discovered in seconds.

Spotting a large wrench, she attacked the machine, smashing things and frantically pulling wires.

The door opened, and a guard burst in.

One more smash crushed a glowing glass tube, causing sparks to spray. This was followed by a small explosion, which didn't hurt her but temporarily blinded her. The machine was dead, and the ever-present pulse of power that filled the institute was gone, leaving an eerie stillness.

She heard angry shouting. Rough hands grabbed her.

"Zarblerg!"

Instantly, her demon appeared.

"Kill them!" she commanded with relish.

Zarblerg tore the throat of the shocked guard who was holding her.

More guards appeared at the door.

"Kill them! Kill them all!" She shrieked.

Zarblerg was noticeably bigger than when she saw him last and had become quite formidable, mercilessly and quickly killing two more guards. An alarm bell began to sound.

They made their way back up to the main level and saw a chaotic scene. Patients and nurses in the common room were running to their rooms to hide, screaming madly or cowering in a corner.

Three more guards attacked, and Zarblerg killed them quickly. Millicent saw one of the girls who had tormented her and stabbed her with her knife.

More guards came, and Zarblerg killed them. The administrator appeared, and Millicent grinned. She turned and ran; Millicent chased her and took her down. She rolled on her back and stared up at Millicent with wide, terrified eyes, who stabbed her in the abdomen repeatedly until her arm began to tire.

There was a lull; all the guards were dead. Millicent rose and said, breathless, "Zarblerg, smash through this window." She motioned to the large windows in the common room. This he did easily.

"Escape with me! You are all free!" she shouted to

the few patients still in the common room.

Then she ran through the opening and along the grass field between the building and the outer wall. Zarblerg helped her over the wall and found herself on the street.

Now, she was free of the institute but was still trapped in the city, and her gray outfit, as well as her hands, were completely covered with blood. She needed to hide quickly. Looking around to get her bearings, she picked a direction to run, the demon on her heels. Luckily, she could see no people in the area.

She spotted a sewer canal, jumped in, and entered a tunnel.

After a time, she stopped, gasping for breath. All was quiet. The water seemed reasonably clean, so she bent and washed the blood from her face and arms.

"Zarblerg, can you lead us to where Aldous lived?"

"Yes, mistress."

"Oh, Zarblerg, I am so glad to see you!" She was so happy she embraced him.

Zarblerg was puzzled, not understanding what a hug was or its purpose.

With Zarblerg in the lead, they went deeper into the catacombs and, in an hour, reached Aldous' former abode. She found some water but no food.

There, she rested and formulated a plan to escape

the city.

"We will leave by train during the night. The roads will be guarded, no doubt. We can hide in a freight train. They should be empty when we leave the city. We will need some food."

"Yes, Mistress," turning as if to obey her command.

Millicent imagined the demon bringing her dead rats and exclaimed, "No! We will make due."

"I should cast a spell to change my appearance. Let's see, my hair black, and my eyes brown. I will need a change of clothing too. Zarblerg, go find Benedict and bring him to the crypt. Have him bring a change of clothes, some food, and money. Oh, and a stiletto. Oh, and a map of the land south of the city."

"Mistress," it said and disappeared.

She attempted the spell, but the magic would not come. It was as if she were still under the influence of the spell dampener. Screaming in frustration, she tried again. With great difficulty, it worked.

"I can't even cast a simple illusion spell. What have they done to me!" she exclaimed, wringing her hands in exasperation.

Now a brunette, Millicent made her way to the surface, glad that the markings she made to lead her there remained.

She waited impatiently inside the crypt. An hour

later, the door creaked open, and Benedict appeared. She was surprised at how much older he looked. His hair was peppered with gray, his eyes were a little hollow, and he seemed thinner.

She stepped toward him and punched him in the gut. He groaned and doubled over. "How much?" she asked, glaring at him.

"What?" he croaked.

"How much did they pay you to betray me?"

"Ah." He reddened slightly and looked down. "I am sorry about that. If it makes you feel any better, your demon has been torturing me for the past few months."

She considered killing him then and there but knew he could be of use to her in the future.

"Never mind, we'll discuss it later. Give me my things."

He handed her a sack.

"Go now; Zarblerg will summon you when I need you next."

Benedict nodded, then left.

She changed and headed to the train station, trying to get to the less traveled streets. Her clothing was black with a hood, a style worn by working-class women, and she attracted no attention.

A few trains were at the train yard, but only one seemed to be preparing to leave. She told Zarblerg to materialize inside one of the cars and open the door for her. A few workers were lingering around, and she would have to make a quick dash to avoid being seen. She jumped inside the train and was about to close the door when she heard a shout.

She drew her stiletto and held her breath. Someone was approaching on the gravel. There was a pause; then the door was closed. With relief, she realized she wasn't seen, only the open door. The car was empty and pitch dark, so she sat against the wall and waited.

CHAPTER 33

Millicent must have fallen asleep, and the next thing she knew, she was awakened by the train lurching forward. The idea of the voyage excited her. She had only left the city a few times with her father and remembered the country with some fondness, but then visions of her father being murdered intruded her mind, and she became angry, and her thoughts turned to fantasies of revenge.

She summoned Zarblerg and bade him tell her everything that occurred when she was locked up. The demon was not a good storyteller, and she had to stop him frequently to go into more detail. The tortures he visited upon Benedict gave her squeals of delight and eye-watering laughter. She was impressed by how much he learned since she was gone and touched by how loyal he had been.

After a few hours, she could see some light filtering through the door and opened it a crack to see where she was. It was dawn, and she could see trees, fields of crops, and beautiful green pastures. The city's smog was gone, and everything looked clean and fresh. Looking at her map, she saw that they would cross a river soon, and that was when she had to abandon the train. The prospect of jumping off the moving train worried her; she hoped she would survive without injury.

Later, the train began to slow, and the sound of the train on the tracks changed. They were on the bridge, the river far below. She prepared to jump, waiting until she passed over the bridge. Luckily, the train was still moving slowly, and she jumped off and rolled down the slope with only a few bruises.

"Zarblerg."

The demon appeared. "Try to find me a boat on this river, but don't be seen. If you find one, bring it to me. I will wait here."

After a time, she heard the sound of rowing, and a small rowboat appeared around the bend in the river. She giggled at the incongruous sight of Zarblerg rowing.

"How did you learn how to row Zar?"

"I consumed the brain of the boat's owner. He knew a lot about the river."

"Oh, go you. Well, you better hide and let me row. If you are seen, it will attract attention."

The boat floated down the river, and Millicent was enchanted by the green pastures dotted with livestock, the fields of wheat, and charming little farmhouses. She never thought much about the country, thinking of it as dirty and dull, but after her time inside the walls of Bedlam, she found herself enjoying the fresh air and quiet. She saw many cows but very few people. Fewer still seemed to notice her in the river, but those that did waved and smiled as she passed, which puzzled her.

When the sun was getting low, she spotted some ruins in the distance, and as she got closer, she became convinced that it was her castle, Rabe Hold. Her heart thudded with excitement.

The vegetation was thick, and it was challenging to find a clear path to the ruins, but after some searching and crouching down to avoid low branches, she could row into a section of the castle itself. She passed through many cobwebs, which stuck to her face and drove her mad. It looked ancient, and what she could see was entirely ruined, but she hoped there would be some livable sections. Vines and moss covered much of the masonry. In some places, fully grown trees had rooted into the walls themselves, as well as other kinds of weeds.

She left the boat to explore on foot and found she was among the ruins of the outer wall. After scrambling up with the help of some vines, she reached a section atop the wall that was intact for a better view. Most of the outer wall was demolished or completely gone, but within was the main keep, of which at least some sections seemed intact, as well as a tower at the far end of the complex. She climbed down from the wall and into a courtyard overgrown with vegetation. A rustling sound startled her, and she grabbed for her stiletto, but then she saw the horns and white whiskers of a goat. It was wholly unconcerned with her, only interested in the sweet grass it was grazing. More goats appeared, making "baa" sounds. She laughed.

"Hey Zarblerg. Do you know how to cook?"

"I have killed and consumed several people with this skill, yes."

"Good, can you kill and cook one of these goats?"

"Mistress."

She continued her exploration, thrilled at exploring the ancient structure that was her birthright. Nestled within the inner walls was a stately rectangular keep, its presence commanding and resolute. The entrance way into the keep stood open and forlorn, its door long since vanished. It led to a small storage room, bare of anything useful. In the room, she struggled to open a creaky door, and as it groaned ajar, she stepped into a dimly lit hallway. Continuing her exploration, she found many rooms with intact floors, walls, and ceilings. Up on the second floor, a few of the walls were crumbling, but the rooms that were intact were in decent shape and could be comfortable with some cleaning. Some contained beds and furniture, and she chose the best one for her bedroom.

By this time, the sun was about to set. She could smell the goat cooking. It smelled delicious, especially since she had not eaten for a couple of days. Zarblerg appeared and handed her a cooked leg of goat, still steaming.

"Okay, thank you. You may put it down. Can you light a fire in this fireplace?"

Soon, she was full and content, and a small fire warmed the room. For the first time in many months, she felt safe. She went to bed and instantly fell asleep despite the dust everywhere.

When she woke in the morning, she felt refreshed and commanded Zarblerg to begin cleaning the rooms, starting with her bedroom.

There was much work to do, but there were more rooms she wanted to explore before beginning the renovation in earnest. And she wanted to find the items her father promised would be there. On the second floor, she found a library. Most of the books were missing, but she was thrilled to see several volumes underneath a collapsed bookshelf.

The top floor of the keep mostly had rooms with holes in the ceiling, rotted floors, and birds living in them. There was only one area left that she had yet to explore: the tower, which was once connected to the keep by a chamber but had long since fallen into ruins.

She had more of the goat, so she paid some attention to the kitchen and had Zarblerg clean it out. She sorted out the objects she wanted to keep from the ones not worth saving and began making a mental list of things to buy. She wondered if she could find a cook and staff to help from some village nearby. Zarblerg could sweep, clean out garbage, and cook but was far too brutish to be a house servant.

She found a small chamber that was flooded, perhaps a cistern, but with the roof long gone. She undressed and took a bath.

It was dark again by this time, and she returned to the bedroom. After trying a simple light spell, which failed, she realized her time in the Bedlam Institute with the spell dampener had significantly eroded her magic skills. She resolved to renew her magic studies with vigor. She found a box of candles and used them to light her way to the bed chamber. On the way, she noticed a faint light coming from the top of the tower.

"Zarblerg, there is someone in the tower."

"Shall I kill it for you, Mistress?"

"No, let me see who it is, but stay close by in case I need you."

She quietly found her way to the tower, navigating around great piles of rubble. It was once joined to the castle but was now standing alone, the hall attaching it to the castle in ruins. The tower itself appeared intact all the way to the top.

Drawing her stiletto, she opened the door at the bottom of the tower, noting that the stairwell was fairly clean of debris and dust. After extinguishing her candle, she quietly climbed the stairs, spiraling upward and going toward a faint glow at the top. Every 15 steps or so was a landing, all empty and unused. Finally, as she neared the top and rounded the corner, she could hear a slight scratching coming from the room. Peeking inside, she saw an old man sitting with his back to her. He was sitting at a desk with a candle and writing feverishly in a book. The man was tall and looked ancient, with slight wisps of white hair hanging down from his mostly bald head. His robes were gray and dirty but seemed in good condition otherwise.

Sensing no danger, she lowered her stiletto and took a few steps into the room. The man didn't notice. She wondered if he was deaf. After watching him for a few moments, she shouted, "Hey! What are you doing in my castle?"

He jerked violently in surprise and spun around with wide eyes behind thick spectacles. "Ah, Regina. What are you doing here this time of night?"

She was about to ask who Regina was but then decided to have some sport. "I am not Regina. I am her ghost, and I am here to murder you."

"Bosh! Stop jesting, Regina, I have work to do. Leave the supplies and go."

Perplexed and disappointed that the old man was not afraid, she stood there for a time, then left, deciding he was harmless and to deal with the situation later.

Lying in her bed, she tried to remember her father's exact words. He said, "There will be things there that you will find useful, but they are hidden, and you must use your wits to find them."

The books were indeed helpful. Several volumes contained magic, and some told the history of Rabe Hold and the surrounding areas. But there was no money and nothing hidden that she had yet found. In the morning, she resolved to find the treasure.

CHAPTER 34

Millicent went to the basement to search once again. There was a wine cellar, with several bottles still full, a pantry with shelves and barrels that once contained food but were long since eaten by rats, and some storage rooms with broken furniture and a wide assortment of primarily useless junk. In one room was a bare shelf, and Millicent noticed the shelf and floor below it were less dusty than one might expect. The shelf was also constructed differently from the others and looked newer.

She grabbed the shelf and shook it. To her surprise, it moved easily. She dragged it away from the wall and saw a strange clockwork mechanism made of metal, shiny like new. It looked something like a clock but had three hands. The largest one was made of silvery metal, and the two smaller ones of brass. The large hand was encircled by markings that were the months of the year, and within the months, smaller markings indicated the days. Inside that band were two bands, which she deduced indicated the phases of the moons. The outer moon band was most likely Mitra since it was pictured larger, and the inner one was Petra. To the right of the mechanism were three handles placed waist high and side by side a foot apart. The whole mechanism was mounted on a metal plate, about four feet high and the same wide. The plate was bordered all around by more metal about an inch wide. It looked to her like a gigantic safe.

Millicent stared at it for a while, trying to understand. Her father liked puzzles; they would solve them together when she was younger. She tried to move the large hand. It spun easily. Then she tried to turn one of the handles. When she did, it made a clanking sound and broke off, falling to the ground with a clang. She deduced that she needed to rotate the hands to a certain combination, then turn the handle, and if she was wrong, the handle would break, and she would be left with one less guess. Now, only two remained.

The answer was most likely a date. The large hand would indicate the month and day of the year, and the combination of moon phases would determine which year that date fell. But what date would her father choose? Then she remembered exactly what he said to her. "You always loved puzzles, ever since the day you were born."

Of course! It was her birth date. It was a pastime among ones her age to determine one's horoscope based on the phases of the moons when they were born, but she didn't place as much stock in it as most of her age. Her astrological sign was called Ophiuchus – the Serpent Bearer and was supposed to indicate one who was willful, stubborn, and impulsive – sclerare!

Carefully, she moved the large hand to the fifth marking of the month of Childas. Her moon signs were waxing crescent Mitra and waning gibbous Petra, and she moved the inner hands to those positions. Holding her breath, she turned one of the two remaining handles. Again, it fell out.

"Fanculo!" she exclaimed out loud. She was sure it was her birthday. Squinting, she looked over the dials. The Mitra dial was a little off, so she fixed it. Holding her breath, she turned the last handle.

This time, she heard a click, and the handle remained secure. She tried to pull, and the door easily swung out.

Her eyes widened at the treasure. There were several sacks, some papers, books, and several small vials. One of the sacks was filled with silver coins. The other was filled with gold coins. And a small sack filled with precious gems.

She was rich and had no need to rely on Benedict or Zarblerg to steal for her. The papers were ancient and included what appeared to be the deed to Rabe Hold. The books were spell books, and she was delighted to see that one was written by her father himself. She scrutinized the vials. They were ancient-looking clay vessels the size of a thumb, sealed with wax. Faintly scrawled on the bottle was a word in the ancient language of Rathberg, the language used for magic; the word meant "healing."

"A healing potion," she said to herself, "These might come in handy someday."

Millicent had breakfast of leftover goat while admiring the fine gemstones. After breakfast, she summoned Zarblerg and sent him to find a stone mason to kill and gain his knowledge.

When the demon returned, she had him start working on fixing the bridges and rebuilding the ruined sections of Rabe Hold. The demon was not particularly skilled due to its clumsy hands, but it did an adequate job. She instructed him to prioritize the sections of the castle she used most and scavenge material from the outer wall, which was beyond repair.

Later in the day, she heard someone walking in the courtyard. She hid and peeked out a door. It was a tall woman, neither young nor old, with long red hair, wearing rough peasant clothing and carrying a basket. She was heading for the tower. Regina, she presumed.

I don't look anything like her; that old man must be crazy, she thought to herself.

Regina didn't stay long, and Millicent watched her leave with her basket empty. On a whim, she decided to follow her.

The woman left through the main gate and continued past the road into a small path in the forest. After a mile, they walked along the border of some farmland. After another mile, they entered a dark, more ancient-looking forest, Millicent always keeping just out of sight.

Suddenly, as she passed a large tree, she was grabbed and felt a blade at her throat. She froze.

"Why are you following me?" a female voice said.

"I own the castle you were trespassing in, you stupid bitch."

Regina seemed to hesitate and lowered the blade slightly. Millicent took the opportunity, grabbing her arm and flipping the woman around and down while drawing her own blade, a move she frequently practiced with Benedict.

"I have a blade, too," Millicent said, standing over her, smiling.

"Indeed, you do." She smiled at Millicent for several moments, which put her at ease, and she lowered her stiletto.

"Come to my hut and have tea with me." She got up and walked on.

Millicent followed.

Soon, they came to a small clearing with a small hut made of wattle and daub with a straw roof. A few goats were milling around, and a small vegetable garden was enclosed in a fence. She entered the hut, and Millicent warily followed. Inside, it was very dark and smelled of fresh hay and herbs.

Without speaking, Regina rekindled, blew on some glowing embers in the fireplace, and put on a pot of water. She smiled again and motioned for Millicent to sit on a rug in the center of the room.

"I thought the owners of the castle were long dead. It has been occupied only by ghosts as long as I can remember."

"Not dead, not quite anyway," Millicent said.

"I hope you don't mind my uncle taking residence. He had nowhere else to go, you see."

"I don't know. What is he doing there?" Despite the woman's friendly and open demeanor, Millicent was on guard, still slightly suspicious.

Regina produced two cups, sprinkled some herbs in them, poured in the hot water, and handed one to Millicent. "He is writing a book of poetry. His masterpiece, he calls it."

"He looks like someone from the Hall of Records," Millicent remarked.

"I don't think so," she laughed.

"Well, why is he out here instead of the city?"

"Ah, I don't know exactly. He is quite hard to understand, but I gather there was some incident, and he was forced to leave Rathberg."

"What sort of incident?" Millicent asked, her curiosity piqued.

"I believe if he returned to the city, he would be arrested. For what, he won't tell me. He is ancient and doesn't always make sense, poor thing."

"What sort of poetry is he writing?"

"Oh, I have no idea. He won't let me see it."

"Interesting," Millicent took a sip of the tea. "Why are you out here all alone?"

"I once had a husband and child, but they were taken by a fever." She took a sip of tea and then added, "But I quite like the solitude."

"Are you a witch?" Millicent asked in all seriousness.

She laughed. "Some in the village would say so, and I know things about herbs and medicine. I can heal."

There was a period of silence while the women sized each other up.

Regina's eyes narrowed, and she said, "By now, the poison in the cup should begin to have taken effect. How do you feel?"

Millicent was about to take another sip but threw the cup away and reached for her knife.

Regina burst out laughing. "Relax, just joking."

Millicent was stunned for a moment and then joined her laughing. Soon, both were laughing so hard that it was difficult to breathe.

They spoke for hours, and Millicent gleaned that Regina indeed knew a lot about herbal medicines and even poisons. She had been taking food and supplies to her uncle twice a week since he first came to the tower about five years ago. Millicent felt comfortable enough to confide that it was she alone who lived in the castle, but she didn't reveal her true background, why she was hiding in the castle, or mention Zarblerg. Regina didn't press on the matter.

The day grew late, and finally, Millicent said goodbye. Regina surprised her with a goodbye embrace.

"When I come with things for my uncle, I will bring some for you," Regina said.

Her warmth was quite disarming.

CHAPTER 35

After a few days of hard work, Millicent had a comfortable bedroom with a nice bed and couch, a clean and usable kitchen, and a tidy library. She decided it was time to summon Benedict and have him bring some luxuries from the city. She made a list of items for him to bring, including clothing, soap, kitchen utensils, and pots, and then gave the list to Zarblerg. The demon was instructed to bring Benedict the list and lead him to the castle.

Late in the afternoon on the second day, she heard a wagon approaching and saw Benedict in a one-horse farmer's wagon rolling into the courtyard. He stopped, and Zarblerg became visible atop the wagon.

She was so excited about the clothes that Millicent ran to the trunk without even a word for Benedict and bade the demon carry the trunk to the bedroom. The clothing was mainly on the drab side, but she was nonetheless pleased to have more options. She remembered Benedict and the other things and came back down.

"You are sure you weren't followed?" She was curt

with him, having decided to not kill him but neither to forgive him.

"Of course," he replied.

"Next time, bring some more colorful clothing. Go to Zandinas on Market Street."

"I will need more money," he said flatly.

"Well, steal some. Wait, on second thought, here." She took out a few gold coins from her purse. "You can have these. It would be inconvenient if you were caught."

He said something under his breath and then turned to leave.

"And stop looking so glum. I've decided that I won't kill you."

Regina returned later that day carrying two baskets containing freshly baked bread, fruits and vegetables, and a hunk of goat cheese. One basket she gave to Millicent.

Millicent smelled the delicious bread and said, "Thank you. I've had nothing but goat since I've been here."

"Come, let me introduce you to my uncle Theobald," Regina said cheerfully.

Millicent followed her up the tower where the old man was busily writing.

"Uncle, this is my friend Millicent."

He turned around on his stool and squinted through his glasses. "Don't play tricks on an old man.

I can see that it's Annabelle. How are you, dear?" he asked kindly.

Upon hearing that name, Millicent felt a strange shiver down her spine. Her mother's name was Annabelle. Her father often said she looked very much like her mother, and a portrait of her in the family estate made Millicent feel it was true. Was it possible he knew her mother, or was it pure coincidence, a mad old man's fancy?

"No, Uncle, this is Millicent. She owns the castle but says you may stay here as long as you want," Regina chirped.

"Indeed she does, indeed. Playing tricks on an old man should be ashamed..." He turned around and continued to mutter to himself.

"Can I see the work you have done on the castle?" Regina asked.

"Yes, okay," she said distractedly. She decided it must be a coincidence and resolved to forget about it.

Climbing back down the stairwell, Regina said, "Don't mind my uncle. He sometimes has moments of confusion, but he is always gentle."

"Was he always like that?"

"No, as far as I recall, he was quite sharp when he was younger. I didn't see him much growing up."

Millicent gave Regina a tour of the castle, who was amazed by her progress, thinking she had done it all alone, even though Zarblerg had really done most of the heavy work.

CHAPTER 36

That evening, Millicent had a dream in which she relived something that happened when she was twelve. She attended a party at her friend Petrina's estate. The estate was ancient and covered with ivy, perfect for spooky games, so they hired an Omen Diviner and a Ghost Summoner.

First, they played Snapdragon in the kitchen because it was the spookiest room with its rough stone walls. A platter was placed on the table, filled with brandy and raisins, and lit on fire. The blue flame gave the girls a ghost-like appearance. As soon as it was lit, the girls sang the Snapdragon song and began picking flaming raisins out of the fire. It was said whoever picked the most raisins would be the first to wed. Millicent liked popping the still flaming raisin in her mouth and trying to blow flame.

Next, they retired to the parlor, which was a much more opulent room with fine furniture and sumptuous draperies. They took turns sitting at a small table with the Diviner while the other girls watched. The clairvoyant practiced Geomancy, where the girl was instructed to grab a handful of dirt from a bag and toss it onto a special board with markings. Millicent remembered her omen vividly. She was told she would lead an auspicious life filled with many tribulations and triumphs and experience betrayal.

Later in the night, they all held hands around a table, and all lights were extinguished except for a single candle on the table. The Ghost Summoner asked who they wanted him to channel. Petrina suggested Millicent's mother, to her chagrin. When the spell was cast, the medium's eyes rolled back and became completely white, the room became still, and the girls giggling gave way to grave faces.

A voice sounding both near enough to touch yet also vastly distant began to speak, "Millicent..."

Millicent could not remember her mother's voice but somehow knew it was her.

"Answer her," one of the girls whispered.

"Yes, mother," Millicent answered.

"Millicent, so pretty. You look so much like me."

There was a long pause; Millicent was at a loss for words.

The voice then uttered an anguished howl, disturbing the girls so much they almost let go of their hands and broke the circle.

There was another pause, and then the voice began again, this time calm but sad: "I forgive him. Tell him I forgive him. I must go."

The medium began to shake violently, and then his eyes rolled back to normal. The spell was broken. The girls were frazzled but also gleeful. It was an exciting performance. Millicent, however, was deeply disturbed, although she hid that from her friends. Who did she mean to tell he was forgiven?

Millicent never spoke of the incident and had forgotten the entire thing until she had the dream. But she was beginning to believe her mother's death was more of a mystery than her father revealed.

CHAPTER 37

After a week, Millicent was bored with the endless work of restoring the castle and decided it was time to explore the countryside. She used some illusion spells and took on the role of a simple peasant girl, a brunette whom she called Colette, who was returning from Rathberg after visiting her uncle.

She came to the road and picked the direction away from Rathberg. Soon, a wagon came by, heading in her direction. The man tipped his head at her but said nothing. After a mile or two, she came to a hamlet consisting of several cottages with thatched roofs and a few more significant stone buildings.

A man appeared out of the largest building and went off to a tree to urinate. She heard voices inside and entered. There was a large room with tables and a bar on the wall. A handful of people were inside. People glanced at her curiously but didn't seem overly interested. She sat at a table, trying to look like a peasant and not a spoiled rich girl.

A middle-aged woman wearing an apron and

bonnet approached, "Do you need anything, lass?"

Millicent ordered a meal and some ale and observed, trying to decide how much she could trust the villagers.

The idea of being an anonymous peasant girl was novel to her. She was used to being stared at and being the center of attention. After a time, a man at an adjacent table spoke to her; his country accent was thick and difficult to understand. She kept to her story that she was a peasant girl traveling from the city to her small town far away, having visited an uncle in the city and bringing some papers from him to her parents. As evening approached, more people filtered into the tavern. After Millicent mentioned justice officers, the entire room became involved in a lively conversation in which they made their disdain for the Justice Ministry and the city folk well known. She found that they were also very uninformed, having never even heard of the homunculi. In fact, they seemed utterly uninterested in the gossip and goings on in Rathberg.

After a time, she was drunk and found herself laughing and joking with them. A woman began to sing, and the men joined in. She never mingled with common people much, but she decided she liked these simple folk. As she was leaving, the matron of the pub handed her some fresh bread and insisted that she take it without payment. This was astounding to her. Never was anyone in the city that generous. In fact, everyone always seemed to want something from you, and many would steal if they had a chance.

Walking home, she recalled her tenth birthday, when her father took her and some friends on an outing in the country. They rented a villa and played Throw Turnips at the Peasants, in which several peasants were hired to stand still while the children threw turnips at them for points. It never occurred to her that they were people, too, with feelings just like her.

CHAPTER 38

Months passed while Millicent diligently studied her magic, and Zarblerg busied itself restoring the castle. So busy did she keep herself that the days passed quickly, and the season turned to winter.

She spent many hours in the library reading the spell books and practicing with fervent dedication. There was a book of local herbs, which she studied to find and gather reagents for her spells. Her father's spell book was fascinating. She reread it countless times.

Knowing that spell casting requires enormous stamina, she did not neglect physical training. She had a regime of jogging around the castle, practicing archery, and sparring with Zarblerg. Fortunately, the benefit of a demon sparring partner is that she could use a real sword and not worry about hurting him, not permanently, anyway.

Regina would visit twice a week, bringing fresh food and baked goods. They developed a routine of having breakfast in the courtyard, which Millicent enjoyed immensely. Regina was her first actual friend not of her station, but she liked her much more than any of the posh city girls she knew.

One such morning, Regina asked her if she would ever return to the city.

"Yes, someday," she replied tersely.

Regina studied her briefly and said, "Something terrible happened to you in Rathberg, didn't it?"

Millicent was surprised by Regina's intuitiveness. It was as if she could read her mind. She looked down at the ground and frowned.

"Do you want to talk about it?"

"No," Millicent said curtly. She was becoming annoyed.

"Very well, I didn't mean to pry."

CHAPTER 39

Every few weeks, Millicent became bored with the routine and visited the hamlet as Colette, telling them that she had been hired to be a handmaiden by the eccentric noblewoman who lived in the castle whom she called Duchess Arabella. She made up delicious stories about her, that she kept a pet wyvern, how she would have dinner parties with the ghosts that haunted the castle, and about her late nights spent casting terrible spells. The tavern patrons were both fascinated and terrified and seemed very concerned for her, trying to talk her into leaving the Duchess' service, offering her work in the hamlet. Their concern touched her, but she politely refused.

One of the books in the library was a history of Rabe Hold. It began with some general history of Rathberg, how it began as a monarchy, but some 200 years ago, there was a revolution by the city guilds who killed the King and most of the nobility and took control over the government, forming the Ministries and sharing power. This much she knew, having been taught to her by Nicodemus, but then it spoke of her ancestors, who were involved in the coup. One man named Salvadore, her great-grandfather several times back and a powerful magician, was given this castle as a reward for his work in the revolution, but apparently, he had to return to the city after only briefly living in the castle to help run the government, and so the neglected castle fell into ruins.

Another book that she found fascinating was about the Red Plague. About a century ago, a mysterious disease suddenly appeared and raged through the city. A person would wake feeling fine, but a red rash would cover their entire body by the evening, accompanied by a high fever. The victim would become unconscious, and by the following day, most would be dead.

The disease would die down and reemerge every few years, but eventually, it vanished without a trace, although its legacy remained, with the numerous tombstones and memorial plaques around the city and brief mentions in history books.

A brilliant idea came to her. If she could somehow revive the Red Plague, she could infect all her enemies, and they would die a painful death, everyone in the Justice and Tech Ministries. She imagined the Masquerade Gala and the Justice Minister would suddenly turn red and fall down dead, and everyone in the party would panic and run in terror, only to fall in the streets to die.

She fell asleep with sweet dreams of revenge.

CHAPTER 40

The next day, Millicent visited Regina, eager to tell someone about her idea.

Over tea, by a warm fire in the dimly lit but comfortable hut, Millicent explained her plan, "Did you ever learn about the Red Death?"

"Yes, everyone does. Why?" Regina asked.

"Wouldn't it be grand if we could find someone who has it and send them to the city, and all the homunculi and justice officers will get it and die."

Regina started choking on her biscuit, and when she recovered, she said, "Millie, you can't do that. Think of how many innocent people will die."

She crinkled her forehead and thought for a moment, "Yes, of course you are right. It was just a silly notion anyway. No one gets the Red Plague anymore."

Regina regarded her momentarily, then crawled beside her, put her arm on her shoulder, and asked, "Millie, why do you hate the Justice Ministry so much? What happened to you in the city?"

Millicent stared at the ground for a moment,

then answered softly, "They murdered my father."

"The moons! That's horrible. I suspect the Ministry also had something to do with my uncle being cast out of the city. Why did they murder your father?"

Millicent felt safe enough to share more, "My father was the Minister of Magic. The Justice and Tech Ministries plotted together to kill him and take control of the city. They came for me and killed my tutor and butler, but I was able to hide. For a few days at least."

Regina gasped, went over to her pantry, and grabbed a bottle. She poured a little brandy into Millicent's cup.

Millicent continued, "They tortured me and then imprisoned me in the Bedlam Prison. For seven months, I was there until I escaped. My father told me about the castle our family owned, so I came here."

She neglected to speak about her demon, unwilling to reveal all her secrets, even to Regina.

"I suspected you had been through some trauma, but that is terrible. No wonder you want revenge so badly." Regina peered at her intensely with her kind brown eyes.

Millicent was momentarily embarrassed and looked down.

Finally, she said, "I will help you heal."

"Heal? I am well."

"No, you are not. You have trauma."

Millicent was perplexed. People outside the city were so different. She was always taught to keep her feelings to herself and was not used to speaking so honestly about these things. Such was the brutality of life in the city. "I am well, I am happy," she answered.

Regina looked at her deeply.

There was a long pause, and then Millicent added, "They did something to me in Bedlam. Sometimes, I feel like my soul leaves my body."

Regina got up, removed a little bell from a shelf, and sat cross-legged on the rug.

"Sit like me. Close your eyes."

Millicent copied her posture.

"When I ring this bell, you will become completely relaxed," Regina said softly.

The bell tinkled.

"Take in a deep breath. Now breathe out, emptying your lungs entirely. Take full, deep breaths."

Millicent felt silly and began to giggle.

"Imagine yourself standing at the edge of a serene, tranquil lake. Take a step forward, immersing yourself in the crystal clear water with each step. Feel a sense of tranquility wash over you as if the water is carrying away any worries or disturbances. As you continue to walk deeper into the lake, notice how the water becomes even more peaceful and envelops you in a soothing embrace. Feel the weightlessness of your body as you float effortlessly, surrendering to the gentle currents. As you surrender, let go of any resistance or tension within you, allowing peace to flow through every cell of your being."

Millicent began to feel a profound sense of calm and ease.

"Visualize a soft golden light. This light represents the sense of peace radiating from within you and expanding outward, creating a bubble of tranquility around you. As the light grows brighter, feel it, dissolving any lingering thoughts or emotions that disturb your peace. Allow yourself to feel the serenity of this golden light."

After several minutes of silence, Regina rang the bell again, and Millicent opened her eyes.

"How do you feel?"

"Good," Millicent answered sincerely.

"Good. We can do that once or twice weekly or more if you like."

CHAPTER 41

One spring day, the alarm spell Millicent cast to alert her of intruders was activated, causing the sound of bells ringing throughout the castle. From her window, she saw a traveling salesman guiding a donkey cart gingerly approaching from the outer gate. She decided to have some fun and used a spell to create the illusion of a gigantic wyvern that dove down at the man, driving him away so urgently that items fell off the cart in his haste, which he left behind.

Bored from a long day of studying magic, Millicent climbed the tower to see Theobald. He was in his bed, snoring loudly. Feeling naughty, she crept over to his desk and opened the book containing his poem. Her eyes widened. She turned the page. Then another. Every page was filled with a single word —"ananana" repeated over and over again. There were hundreds of pages. Oddly shaken, she quietly left.

The following evening, Millicent was reading one of her father's spell books. She noticed one of the pages was dog-eared. It was for a spell called

Befuddlement. Something in the writing caught her interest. It said the spell would permanently cause someone to lose most of their memory and become simple. One of the side effects was that they could display obsessive behavior, such as repeating the same phrase over and over. It reminded her of Theobald. Could her father have cast the spell on him? For what reason? If they had known each other, it would have explained how he mistook her for her mother. But she had to find out for sure. On the next page was an antidote to the Befuddlement spell. She studied the spell until she was satisfied she knew it cold, then ran down to the tower.

Theobald was still asleep. That was good. If the spell failed, he would not be any the wiser. She chuckled at the irony of that thought.

She completed the spell and felt the familiar sensation of power flowing out of her after a spell was successfully cast.

Theobald coughed in his sleep, then opened his eyes.

Millicent could see the difference immediately in the clearness of his eyes; he was changed.

He blinked several times, staring at Millicent. Then he reached for his glasses and put them on.

"Annabelle? Is that you?"

"No Theobald, I am Millicent, Annabelle was my mother."

"Mother..." He looked down, obviously

bewildered and extremely upset. "No…" He glanced up at Millicent, then back down and began crying. "I'm sorry. I'm sorry. I couldn't save her."

"Come, Theobald, let's go into the castle, I will make you some tea."

They sat in front of a fire in the parlor. He had a blanket around him and was sipping a cup of tea, which she spiked with liquor.

"You look so much like her."

"Please tell me what happened. Why did you say you were sorry?" she asked gently.

"I was butler to your mother's family before she was born. Then, butler to your father as well, after they were married. About a year after you were born, she became ill. Your father took her to all the best healers, but she slowly kept declining. Your father was desperate and began seeking magical remedies, dabbling in the forbidden secrets of necromancy and slowly losing his grip on reality. I tried to get him help, but he refused. Then, one horrible night, she passed. Lucian became like a madman, took her into his study, and locked the door. I heard strange and terrible noises through the night. In the morning, I had fallen asleep and was woken by a loud crashing sound. I ran down to the noise and saw the door to the parlor open and hanging from its hinges as if someone had broken it down. Then I heard a noise in the kitchen and ran over to see your mother standing as if alive but with pallid gray skin like a corpse. She had her hands around the neck of the maid and was strangling her. I was in a state of such shock and terror I couldn't move. Then your father rushed in. He was bleeding badly from his head, and he held a sword."

"'Annabelle!' he cried."

"The maid fell, lifeless, and Annabelle turned. Her eyes were terrible to behold. There was no life there. So terrified was I that I fell backward and lay helpless on the floor."

"Then she... it, spoke, 'Annabelle is gone, I'm in here now!' The voice was raspy and shrill, unrecognizable."

"'I'm sorry, Annabelle, so sorry!' Lucian cried, then attacked it with the sword.

"I must have blacked out and found myself on a couch in the parlor. Lucian gave me liquor, but I was so distraught I couldn't speak."

"He left me alone for a time, then returned. The last thing I remember was watching him cast a spell."

Millicent felt a wave of dizziness wash over her as the revelation hit her. It was unthinkable that her father could have done something so reckless. She delved deep into the recesses of her memories, searching for clues. Her father had always been silent about her mother's death. She'd only ever heard the story whispered by others. Doubt gnawed at her, but deep down, she knew in her heart it had to be true.

After a few minutes Millicent had recovered enough to say, "He cast a spell on you to wipe your memory. But why, did he not think you would ever recover from the shock?"

He sat quietly for a time, his face contorted with emotion, then said, "No, I think he did it because he was afraid someone would find out what happened about his working in necromancy. He had just become Minister, and his position was not yet fully established. Annabelle's father was an important elder in the Ministry and helped Lucian get elected. It could have ruined Lucian's career if he had found out what happened."

Millicent stared into the fire. "He told me she died in childbirth. No one ever spoke of her death. What he did to you was terrible!"

"No, I understand why he did it. He could have killed me, instead he made sure I was taken care of. I was loyal; I wouldn't willingly talk. But if there was an investigation, I am a terrible liar and may well have revealed the secret."

"Sleep now. Tomorrow, we will talk more. You can tell me about my mother." Millicent cast a sleep spell on him and laid him on the couch before the fire. He was shockingly light to pick up, all skin and bones.

Millicent was upset, angry at her father for lying to her and for wiping Theobald's memory, and sad about hearing the details of her mother's tragic death. She couldn't sleep and so took a sleeping draught herself.

CHAPTER 42

In the morning, she went to fetch Regina, eager to tell her that her uncle had been restored. She talked the entire time, telling Regina everything as they returned to the castle.

She and Theobald embraced like they had not met in years, and all three began to talk. Regina revealed that a man came to her to tell her that her uncle was unwell and needed care and that he would be staying in the castle tower. She thought the man was a friend of his, but it was now clear that Lucian had arranged it all.

They asked Theobald what he wanted. He said he wanted to stay in Rabe Hall and resume duty as Millicent's family butler. She agreed but made him promise to do only light work.

"What of your poem?" Regina asked.

"Bah, pure drivel. You can use it to wipe your arse for all I care."

They laughed.

CHAPTER 43

Months passed, then years, and Millicent's eighteenth birthday was only a week away. Theobald served loyally as her butler, and Regina visited often. For the first time in her life, she felt as if she had a proper family.

She was by now highly skilled at magic, mastering spells all but the most powerful of magicians could not cast and some spells even her father had never attempted. She had also grown taller, her face longer and leaner, and her figure more mature.

On her birthday, Regina baked Millicent a cake, and they celebrated with some of the fine wine in the basement.

"If I were back in the city, I would be having my debutante ball now," Millicent said wistfully.

"Sounds boring. This is much more fun," Regina joked.

"True," Millicent answered, but was not convinced.

CHAPTER 44

One late summer day, Millicent was bored, so she decided to venture out as Colette and visit the hamlet. Passing by the tavern, the serving woman waved to her, and Millicent approached.

"The bailiff was here." She rolled her eyes. "He heard that the castle was occupied again and wants to meet the Mistress of the Keep."

"Well, she isn't very friendly, I don't think she will see him," said Colette.

"You told us about her, but he is insistent. He wants to feel important and make nice to the local nobility. He is a fawning lizard, that one."

Millicent continued on her way, deep in thought. If the man appeared, she could kill him, but that would create suspicion, and she wanted to keep a low profile. It sounded like he would not be dissuaded, so she became resigned to meeting him, but as Duchess Arabella, the mad lady of the castle, and having some fun with it.

CHAPTER 45

After a few days, Millicent heard a horse approaching and saw a messenger boy ride through the gate. She met him as Colette and took the written message from the plainly terrified courier, who took off quickly, not wanting to spend another minute in the haunted castle.

It read, "By your leave, the Bailiff of the County of Greenhill requests an audience with Duchess Arabella in one week. He looks forward to a visit with your illustrious presence."

The week passed, and when Millicent heard a team of horses and a wagon approaching, she burst into action, having planned for the event all week.

She cast a glamour on herself to make her appear older and much taller, with long hair as black as a raven. She wore a stately but somewhat old-fashioned black gown that showed off her magically enhanced bosom. A table was prepared in the dining hall with tea and some cakes. The curtains were drawn, and a candelabra of 20 candles provided dramatic lighting.

She waited in the entry hall for a knock, then had

the door magically open. Standing there was a portly man of middle age with a thin mustache. He was grinning officiously.

"Come in, my dear Bailiff." Her voice was deep and stately.

"Please, please call me Archibald."

She held out her hand, which he kissed.

"Come, I have prepared tea."

She motioned for him to sit at one end of the very long table, and she sat at the other end.

"I am at your disposal, Duchess. Ever since I heard of your arrival, I have wanted to come and pay my respects. Indeed, the Baron mentioned that he would also like to meet you." He had to raise his voice slightly more than was comfortable due to the vast distance between them.

"Thank you. Please help yourself," she said, maintaining her monotone.

The Bailiff served himself some tea and cakes. The Duchess remained still and imperious.

"The Baron you say?"

"Yes, Baron Pim. Fine man. He would dearly like to make your acquaintance."

The wind began howling forlornly through some shutters, and a door squealed open somewhere in the castle.

"Indeed," she said.

"I have heard stories that the castle is haunted."

She said nothing.

"Merely stories told by superstitious villagers, no doubt," he added.

"No doubt," she repeated, without emotion.

He loosened his collar; sweat was beading on his balding head.

"I hope you will be staying here with us for awhile."

Millicent whispered something, activating a spell, and the candelabra began floating off the table and, after a few moments, slammed back down. The Bailiff's eyes widened. Next, heavy footsteps seemed to enter the room and approach the table, although no one could be seen.

"What is wrong, Archibald? You look pale."

"Did you hear that?" he exclaimed.

"Hear what?"

"Oh, nothing, perhaps just a bit of indigestion. Not from the tea! I have been unwell..."

"That is a pity," she said.

Just then, a spectral image appeared, a man in archaic clothing carrying an ax; he approached the table menacingly.

The Bailiff, his nominal courage exhausted, having reached the limits of his wits, squealed and rushed out of the room, upturning his chair in the process.

"Please come back soon. You are welcome anytime!" Millicent yelled after him.

Millicent waited until he was outside before bursting into laughter. Zarblerg appeared.

"Well done, Zar. Your footsteps frightened him."

"Thank you, mistress."

"I don't think he will be bothering us again."

A few days later Millicent was surprised to see the messenger boy return. This time the message read,

My dear Duchess. I have heard so many interesting things about you, I beg you to visit me for tea. One week's time would be suitable. My estate is five miles past the hamlet, just off the main road. Signed – Baron Pim.

Millicent was perplexed that the Baron would still want to meet her after her treatment of the Bailiff. She suspected some kind of a trap. But if she refused she feared he would not give up pestering her. She decided to venture out as Colette and discover as much as possible about this Baron. If all else failed she would have to kill him, but that would be a last resort as it would bring unwanted attention from the Justice Ministry.

CHAPTER 46

It was a fine day, and a few miles past the hamlet, she spotted an orchard just off the road and had a notion of scrumping some apples. She was sitting by a tree, enjoying one, when she spotted a farmhouse in the distance. There was a child, and something struck her as unusual, so she went for a closer look.

The boy was about four, had very long hair, wore mere remnants of clothing, and was filthy. He was penned up with the pigs, moved about on hands and knees as if he didn't know how to walk, and made grunting noises like a pig.

A farmer came out with a basket and threw kitchen scraps into the pen. The pigs fought for it and wouldn't let the boy have any.

This mistreatment reminded her of her time in Bedlam, but this was much worse. Enraged, she approached the house and grabbed a broom that was leaning against the door. She entered and saw the farmer and his wife sitting at the dining table.

"Who the hell are you?" he said.

"Who the hell are you to treat your son like that?"

He got up, palpably angry. "None of your damn business, you little wench!" he yelled, rushing forward to grab her.

She struck him hard with the broom on the head, stunning him.

"You're gonna regret that, whore!"

She thrust out with the broom and hit him in the bollocks, followed by a swing to his head, then knee, and he fell. The woman just sat there silently, looking terrified.

She put her foot on his throat and said, "I asked you why you treat your son like that?"

He grimaced at her and began to grab for her ankle, so she hit him again in the head several more times until he was bleeding.

"Stop!" he pleaded, "It ain't my son. The Baron paid me to take him. He's not mine."

"Baron Pim?"

"Aye!"

"Why did he send the boy to you? What did he do?"

"I don't know. I think he is his bastard."

She contemplated killing the man but then looked at the terrified woman and instead cast a sleep spell on him. He would not wake for a full day.

"Fetch the boy, give him a meal, a bath, and clothes. I will soon return," she said to the woman.

She walked toward the hill, passing over it, and saw a large field and a small but stately manor house on the other side. Then, she found a comfortable spot beside a tree to sit and watched the house until dark. To pass the time, she summoned Zarblerg.

"What are we doing here, mistress?"

"We are going to teach a bad man a lesson."

"Like I did with Benedict?" Zarblerg asked.

Millicent laughed, "Yes, much like that."

After the candles in the windows were extinguished, she approached the house. She climbed a trellis to the second floor in the room where she saw the candles that were extinguished last, deducing that was the bedroom. Quietly, she opened the window and saw a large bed with a man and woman sleeping. She cast an illusion of a terrifying half-wyvern, half-man creature above the bed.

"Baron Pim! Awaken!" she says through the illusion, changing her voice to a deep and terrifying tone.

He opened his eyes and became rigid, his eyes wide as plates.

"We are aware of your bastard and the despicable treatment of him. Tomorrow, you are to send for him, acknowledge him, and raise him here as a son."

The door burst open, and a man rushed in with a club, clearly a guard. Zarblerg materialized and quickly tore his throat out, blood spraying all over the bed and the couple's faces, then began consuming him.

"If you do not do this, Baron, we will return and consume you. Do you agree to this Baron?"

"Yes, yes! Please don't hurt us," he pleaded, clearly terrified. His wife had fainted.

"We will return periodically; if the boy is being mistreated, you will pay."

Millicent had no doubt he would keep to his promise.

Walking back home, she summoned Zarblerg again, "Well, Zar, that was fun, wasn't it?"

"Yes, Mistress."

"If the Baron bothers me again I will threaten to go public about his bastard, or perhaps I will just kill him."

"I will help you Mistress."

"Thank you, Zar."

That night, Millicent dreamed she was trapped in the pig pen with the boy, and then she was taken back to the Bedlam Hospital and placed in the electrical torture machine. Morcant was there, grinning, then he pulled down on the lever with a maniacal laugh, and she woke with a start, soaked with sweat.

She had an epiphany.

She had grown complacent, content to

peacefully study magic and restore her castle, which she had grown to love. But occasionally, when she thought about her father or her old life, her thoughts would spiral down into a dark, deep well. The meditation had helped her, but her thoughts of revenge remained buried in her heart. The dream reminded her of her purpose, the thing that kept her going during her time in captivity, the vow she made to her dead father for revenge. Her notebooks scattered across the library contained a detailed plan, but there were gaps and weaknesses; she had to move back to the city to begin in earnest. But first, as a sonata or overture of her main plans, she would destroy the Bedlam Institute.

CHAPTER 47

There was a ferry to the city that stopped close to the village. Millicent boarded in disguise, using mundane, non-magical methods, but it was sufficient to prevent even those who knew her from recognizing her.

The ferry stopped several times and took many hours to reach Rathberg. She was shocked by how much the city had changed. Wires hung everywhere, and new factories had been built, belching more smoke into the air. A massive dam was being constructed upriver from Rathberg. Homonculi were now a common sight, patrolling the streets day and night.

Her plan was simple, requiring only Zarblerg and her, but she always felt the simplest plans were the most foolproof and effective.

Waiting until dark, she went to a remote section of Bedlam's outer wall where she would not be seen. Then, still out of range of the spell dampener device, she cast a transmute spell, which caused a hole in the wall to form, big enough for her and Zarblerg to fit. They passed through and ran across the lawn and looked in the windows to the common room, which was dark and empty.

Looking at Zarblerg, she said, "You know what to do."

The demon ran and bashed through the windows, Millicent following close behind. Hearing shouts from the guards but wasting no time, they ran to the door to the cellar where the spell dampener room was. The locked doors proved no barrier to the demon. They reached the room with the electric chair and then bashed into the room where the generator was. The machinery had been repaired since Millicent's last visit. Millicent found a wrench on the ground and gleefully stuck it into a rotating cog. The machine angrily ground to a stop, followed by a brief pause, and then an explosion which knocked Millicent to her feet. By now, the guards had followed them to the cellar, but Zarblerg was making short work of them. They fought back to the main floor, and she began a spell. Such was the complexity of the spell that Zarblerg had to fight off the guards to keep her from being disturbed during the two or three minutes she was casting. Bristling with magical power, she could feel her entire body vibrating. Then, a release came as the spell was cast, and a pool of fire appeared on the floor, spreading outward in a circle.

"Quick, Zar, open these doors and release the girls!" Millicent gasped, exhausted by the casting of the powerful spell.

By the time the last door was opened, the building was an inferno, but she led the girls out through the broken window onto the lawn. Most seemed bewildered and confused. She recognized few of the girls from her time there.

"Go! You are free! Run through the hole in the wall!" Millicent yelled to them. Some heeded her instructions but many just backed away from her, or held each other for comfort. A few were screaming hysterically.

"Why don't you escape?!" Millicent cried in frustration at the remaining girls.

Finally, she gave up and exclaimed, "Chissenefrega!" Then said to Zarblerg, "Thank you, Zar, I will see you back at the castle."

"Mistress."

She ran for the gap in the wall, only then to realize her clothing was covered in blood. She stripped off her coat and hurried down the street. Already she could hear the fire bells ringing and people stirring. She came to a beggar sleeping in the alley and took his coat, throwing him a coin when he resisted. Spotting a chaise, she flagged him down and asked to go to The Docks. She saw a Justice coach approaching, and began to prepare for a spell, but it continued past, rushing toward the fire. She made it back to her boat and set off. After the city began to recede in the distance she could finally relax.

Millicent arrived home mid morning, exhausted

but satisfied with her night's work. She had finally begun the revenge she craved for so long. Bedlam was no more, and its inmates free, or so she naively thought.

CHAPTER 48

Back in the city, Director Aldebrand was busy interrogating the girls who tried to escape Bedlam. Some had remained free, but most were quickly recaptured.

His life since the coup had been good. He had been promoted from Deputy Director to Director and married the prominent daughter of an important house. He was next in line for the position of Minister, but he would have to be patient for that; Morcant was not inclined to step down just yet.

After speaking to a few witnesses, Aldebrand was sure. It was Lucian's daughter, out of hiding, causing great mischief. He warned Morcant that she was dangerous, but he wouldn't listen – the fool!

After her escape, he had assigned one of his best men to find her, but he failed in every attempt for many years fruitlessly searching in the city. Now, he would have to make her recapture his top priority.

Sitting in his office on the top floor of the Tower of Justice, he spent the remainder of the night pouring through files, reading reports about

Millicent's activity in the Bedlam Institute, the bloody escape aided by her demon, her subsequent disappearance, and the numerous sightings and rumors over the years, none of which bore fruit. His instincts told him she was no longer in the city. It was beyond the city that they would resume the search.

In the morning, Gumarich was going through a stack of reports detailing crimes committed in the County Greenhill, a region south of the city. After several hours, one report caught his attention. A pig farmer reported being terrorized by a young girl with black hair, who cast a sleep spell on him. He took the report to Aldebrand's office.

"Well done, Gumarich. It must be her despite the hair color. How many lunatic teenage female magicians can there be? She must have dyed her hair. It is in this region that we will narrow our search.

CHAPTER 49

Millicent continued with the next step of her plan, which involved paying a visit to her old home.

Wearing tight black clothing, a black balaclava, and a backpack, she stood in the alley next to her house, looking up. There was a drainpipe she used to climb down as a girl when she wanted to sneak out without anyone seeing her leave. She climbed about twenty feet to the little hallway window and emerged into the back stairwell to her apartment. She noted how much smaller it seemed than how she remembered. She came to her door and tried to open it. Locked. No matter, she could easily pick it, having practiced her lock picking on the same lock a hundred times. Taking out a small vial from her pack, she oiled the hinges to ensure the door would not squeak. Silently, she opened the door and stepped inside the dark room where she had spent so much time. The windows had new curtains, which blocked most of the light. She took some time for her eyes to adjust to the dark, standing silently and listening. Her bed was still there, in the same place. The decor was much different; stodgy, boring, bourgeois. She saw two shapes in the bed and heard some soft snoring. Hatred burned in her heart at seeing two strangers sleeping in her bed, bigwigs from the Justice or Tech Ministries, or their kin, no doubt, here in her family home obtained by theft and murder. She crept up to the bed and drew her stiletto. She could see the people clearly now. It was a middle-aged couple. Quickly placing her hand on the woman's mouth and slashing her throat, she was able to kill her without waking the man. Next, she did the same to the man, who struggled but was also dispatched quickly. She collected their blood in some vials she had brought. The door to the top floor was also locked, but she easily picked it. The room was fairly well lit by the moons shining through the glass ceiling. There were boxes and old furniture all around. *They were using this as a storage room!* she scoffed to herself.

Clearing a circle on the floor, she prepared for the summoning spell, took the items out of her backpack, and arranged the sulfur and candles. This spell was a little more involved than her first summoning of Zarblerg because she was attempting to summon a specific demon... her fathers'.

There was no guarantee it would come, although she had been diligently studying her demonology texts and could now be considered an expert.

The spell was completed, and the air grew chill.

"Pythomon, I summon you. I am Millicent of the House of Ravens. You served my father, Lucian. I would speak to you."

A presence coalesced out of the smoke.

Slowly, it materialized. It appeared like a large, powerfully built man with pallid white skin, hairless, and straight horns jutting out of his forehead.

"Speak then," it said in a calm voice, so deep she felt the sound in her chest.

Its power was manifest, and she had to fight to keep calm and not show fear, as that could be fatal. "How was my father captured?"

"His underling Ambrosius betrayed him and lured him to a place where magic would not work, and he could not summon me." The creature sounded angry.

"I knew it!" she added, "How did my father create the magic-dampening crystal?"

"I do not know."

"Cavoli! Okay, how can I kill all the homunculi?"

"Those creatures are already dead."

"What? Damn, you are not much help. Where are the rest of the magicians from the Magic Ministry? Were they all killed?"

"Some were killed, many were imprisoned."

"Where?"

"The place is called Nightstone." Suddenly, its voice changed and sounded just like her father's: "Let me out, Milli. I will be your demon familiar. I will take many souls and help you with your dreams of vengeance."

She was taken aback and struggled to keep her composure, feeling the demon trying to submit her to its powerful will. "No. I already have a demon."

It began to laugh; a cruel laugh incongruous with its sinister voice. "That impling? It was the weakest demon in the underworld. How could it help you?" It laughed some more, its derision eroding her confidence and resolve.

"Nevertheless, it is my demon, and it has indeed helped me."

"Release me!" it commanded.

She spoke its name, helping to again bind the demon to her will: "Pythomon. Go now. Do not return unless summoned. By your laws, you must obey."

The demon dematerialized, and Millicent exhaled in relief, exhausted by the experience. But she had one more task before returning to the castle.

Benedict was awakened suddenly by a voice coming from inside his room.

"I will kill you," a strange voice said.

Benedict nearly fell out of the bed in surprise.

Millicent burst out laughing.

Sitting up in bed, blinking, his eyes focused on the small figure in front of him, still wearing all black. "You! Moons, you scared the shit out of me!"

She kept laughing.

"How did you get in here?"

"I picked the locks, you fizgig," she said playfully.

He put his feet down, still sitting on the bed, and ran his fingers through his hair, "What do you want?" he said, calmer now.

"I need you to purchase an estate for me in the city."

He squinted up at her. "Me? Why me?"

"I can't believe I'm saying this, but I trust you."

He opened a flask from his nightstand and drank a swig. "What do I know about estates?"

"It's easy; just go to an agent and tell them what you want."

"Well, what do you want?"

"Something fairly modest, about ten rooms. In the regency district but in the part closer to Ophidian Tower."

"Is that all? Sounds expensive."

She threw him a sack containing gold and precious gems.

"Do I get a commission?" he asked, slightly tentatively.

She felt a rush of anger and was about to say something salty to him but reconsidered, remembering reading in a book that it is good to reward subordinates sometimes.

"Alright, five percent," she said, turning to leave.

"And don't fuck it up. I know where you live," she added before disappearing through the door.

Traveling all night, Millicent returned to the castle at dawn and fell immediately asleep, exhausted from her busy night.

CHAPTER 50

A coach from the Justice Ministry rolled into the village courtyard. Driving was an officer, and beside him sat a homunculus. From out of the coach came a mid-level justice officer. The matron of the pub was outside washing linen. Several eyes from inside the tavern stared from the windows. The homunculi were a spectacle not seen in the village.

The officer told the woman, "You there, gather the villagers. I wish to address them."

She regarded the officer coldly, wiped her hands on her apron, and disappeared into the building. After a few moments, several people filed out, wearing stern expressions that revealed their distaste for the Justice Ministry. A few others came from elsewhere, attracted to the commotion.

The officer spoke, "The Justice Ministry is looking for a dangerous criminal. It is a girl of eighteen, of short stature, with long blonde hair and blue eyes. She may have dyed her hair black. Despite her appearance, she is extremely dangerous. She is mad and has killed multiple citizens. A reward of four hundred ducats is offered for information leading to her arrest. If anyone has seen this girl, come forward."

There was a long, tense silence. The villagers did not associate the brunette girl they knew as Colette with the description provided, but even if they had, they would not have said a word, at least most wouldn't have.

"Very well. If anyone hears anything tell your local magistrate." The officer returned to his coach, and they rode off.

However, a man watching from behind a fence did make a connection to Colette and the recently reoccupied castle, and his greed far exceeded his scruples about not squealing on a fellow country dweller. He stealthily ducked behind a building and ran, intending to intercept the officer on the road outside the village.

The coach stopped, and the officer came out. With his hat in his hand, the man spilled what he knew.

"Thank you, citizen. The Ministry is grateful." He tossed a gold coin to him. "If this Colette is who we are hunting, you will be rewarded."

The coach turned around and sped back to the castle.

Millicent was studying her magic when the wards alerted her to an intruder coming to the castle. From the second-floor window, she could see a Justice Ministry coach rolling into the courtyard.

Quickly, she cast a spell to adopt the appearance of the tall and dark Duchess and walked outside.

The sight of the homunculus disturbed her greatly, reminding her of the day she was caught, but she hid it well and maintained a serene and dignified expression.

The officer exited the coach and bowed, "My apologies, madam. I will not take much of your time. The Ministry is seeking a girl of eighteen of short stature with long blonde hair and blue eyes for numerous serious crimes. Have you seen anyone by this description?"

Her heart pounded, but she stayed calm and answered, "No, Officer, I have not."

The officer hesitated. "Do you have servants here?"

"Only my butler, but he is an old man."

"Pardon, but I have been told a girl serves here who is named Colette, who resembles this person."

Inside, Millicent fumed. Someone from the village must have betrayed her.

"Yes, Colette worked here but has been gone for two months now. She returned to her village to take care of her ailing parents. Furthermore, she is older, taller, and darker than the description of your suspect."

"I see. Well, I am sorry for the intrusion."

He returned to the coach and was inside for a

moment but then exited; also exiting was an older man wearing the Tech Ministry's robes and holding a large wooden box.

"I beg your indulgence, but my colleague insists on showing you this gadget of his," the justice officer said politely.

The Tech man placed it on the ground and removed the top, revealing a glass globe. On the side of the box was a crank, which he began turning vigorously. The box made a whirring sound, and the glass globe began to glow, first faintly, then more brightly as the whirring grew louder and louder, and what looked like little lightning strokes flashed inside.

She backed off, sensing danger. In a heartbeat, she felt the magic drain from her, and the illusion spell was gone, revealing a short, young, blonde girl with blue eyes where the Duchess once stood. To have one's magic dispelled was a deeply disturbing experience for a spell caster, a dreadful violation of an intimate nature. The shock instantly threw her mind back into the disassociated state that she experienced when she was drugged in the Bedlam Institute.

The courtyard burst into chaos, with many things happening simultaneously.

The chief officer furiously barked orders to arrest the girl.

The driver leaped from the vehicle, along with

the homunculus, who also leaped down, though more slowly and stiffly.

Theobald appearing in the courtyard, shouted, "See here now! Leave this young lady alone. She has done nothing wrong, you villains!"

Millicent, despite being stunned, called for Zarblerg. "Kill them!" she shouted in rage. Luckily, he was already on this plane, and no magic was needed for him to hear and run over.

Zarblerg tore the driver apart before he even saw it. The officer drew a sword and faced off with the demon while the homunculus advanced on Millicent, slowly but inexorably. Theobald happened to be in the way, and the creature shoved him aside as effortlessly as a stalk of wheat. Her stiletto was drawn, but she knew better than to let the creature get close enough to grab her, so she turned and ran back into the castle.

The officer thrust expertly with his sword, and Zarblerg was impaled where its heart should have been, but the demon did not even flinch due to not possessing a heart. The demon calmly pulled the man closer, driving the sword in deeper, then tore out the stunned and terrified man's throat.

Seeing this, the terrified Tech man leaped to the driver's seat and whipped the horses, frantically racing off, kicking up dust and torn grass.

Zarblerg rushed into the castle to find his mistress. Millicent ran to the third floor of the keep, a plan in her mind, with the homunculus close behind. She navigated around the rotted floorboards and was now cornered in a room. The monster followed, heedless of the obviously dangerous floor, and with its prey almost within grasp, fell through the rotted floorboards down to a room below. Zarblerg appeared next to her, looked down, and saw the creature below, still moving, then jumped down to it.

"Wait, Zarblerg, don't kill it. Just immobilize it!"

Zarblerg obeyed and got the creature into a bear hug, the demon's strength surpassing even the homunculus, preventing it from moving.

Quickly, Millicent fetched some rope and tied it securely.

"Take it to the cellar. Make sure it can't escape."

"Mistress."

She returned to the courtyard and saw two corpses but no coach or Tech man. Theobald was also on the ground, unmoving. The spell dampener had ceased working.

"Zarblerg! Kill the man that escaped and bring the coach back here! Quickly!"

Crouching down, she realized the old man was dead, his frail body broken by the brutal strength of the homunculus. Furious, she kicked the corpse of the officer. Not satisfied, she ran off to find a stout stick to smash the box with but then reconsidered, thinking the gadget could be helpful in the future, so she stored it in the cellar instead.

She waited, pacing nervously, her mind still partially clouded by the recurrence of the fugue state, worried that the entire justice force would descend on her at any moment.

After some time, Zarblerg returned with the coach. She peeked inside and saw the Tech man, his head hanging loose due to a broken neck.

"Did anyone see?"

"No, mistress."

"Thank the moons."

"Thank you moons," the demon repeated.

"I didn't mean… Oh, never mind."

She felt shaken, having her refuge discovered and violated, and was having difficulty concentrating.

She knew she had to dispose of the bodies in such a way as to deflect suspicion from the castle and make sure no one else knew of their visit to Rabe Hold.

"Zarblerg, fetch Benedict. Tell him to come quickly. I need his help. Make him hurry."

Zarblerg was back in a few minutes, having quickly delivered the message.

"He is coming?"

"Mistress."

"Now take Theobald to his room, gently place

him in his bed, and cover him with a sheet."

"What am I going to tell Regina?" she said aloud to herself.

Benedict did indeed hurry and reached the castle by nightfall, riding a fast horse all the way from the city. He quickly appraised the situation and took control.

"I will take the coach to a dangerous part of the road and make it look like a robbery. Take everything of value. Demon, load the bodies back into the carriage. I just hope no one sees me driving this thing."

"Wait! What bandits tear the throats out of their victims with their teeth?" Millicent said.

"Well, got a better plan, princess?"

She pointed to the Tech man. "Tear out this man's throat, Zarblerg. Leave them far past the village in the forest along the side of the road. Make it look like wolves attacked them; the horses bolted, and they crashed. Let the horses loose to run off."

She climbed into the coach, searched, and came out with a book.

"What is that?" asked Benedict.

"A log book. They were looking for Colette. I only use that name in the village. Someone from the village betrayed me. Perhaps they wrote down his name."

She flipped through the pages.

"It is a list of places they have searched for me."

"Does it mention the name of the informant?" Benedict asked.

"No," she pouted.

"I have to find out who informed against me. Otherwise, I will never be safe," she continued.

"Well, unless you know how to question the dead, I don't see how we can find out," Benedict said.

"I know! Zarblerg, if you eat someone, you know everything they knew, right?"

The demon answered, "Yes, but only if I consume them immediately after death; these creatures are too long dead."

Millicent kicked the corpse of the Tech man in frustration.

"There is another way to question the dead, mistress."

They both turned to Zarblerg wide-eyed, waiting for him to explain.

After a few moments, she said, "How can you question the dead, Zarblerg?"

"I can travel to the plane where the dead go after they are killed and before they move on to the final place."

"Amazing!" Benedict exclaimed.

Millicent was awe-struck. "And you can question him? Wait, how will he speak without a throat?"

"Humans arrive in their spirit form. They do not need a throat to speak. If I can find him, it is a large place."

"Go then. Find the chief officer and find out the informant's name or at least his description."

"Mistress."

She turned to Benedict. "Go. Stage the accident. Make it look good."

"Mistress," he muttered under his breath.

Some hours later, Benedict returned on foot. "I crashed the coach, let loose the horses, and placed the bodies as to look like they were attacked by animals. I don't know if it will fool the Justice men, though."

"Don't be so pessimistic!" she yelled, her nerves strained.

"May I go now?"

"Yes, go back to the city," she said curtly.

He turned and mounted his horse.

"And thank you," she said more softly without looking at him.

He stared at her, amazed for a moment, then rode off.

She was too worried to sleep, so she read the logbook from the beginning. It mainly concerned her and the search for her, as well as a list of the people questioned and places searched. Lucinda the Red was interrogated, and tortured until she died, but, of course, she knew nothing. There was no mention of her escape by train. Iin fact, all the searching was done in the city. Numerous false sightings of her were noted, which caused her great amusement. In the last few days, the search was widened to include the territory beyond the city. This calmed her considerably as they had no inkling of where she might be but merely came to the village in the normal course of their search, or so she thought.

CHAPTER 51

At last, after a few hours, Zarblerg popped in beside Millicent.

"Well! What happened?"

"I found the leader. He did not want to speak to me, but I threatened to trap him there if he did not speak, although I did not possess that power. I was very clever."

"And…?"

"He said the man's name was Rhudolf, and he is tall and gaunt. He said that he paid him a gold coin."

"I think I know him. He comes to the tavern sometimes! You have done well, Zarblerg, thank you."

Millicent dressed in close-fitting black trousers and shirt and rushed off to the village, creeping behind the tavern without being seen and peeking in the back window. Rhudolf was there, drinking some of his reward money, no doubt. She found a spot in some bushes where she could watch the door to the tavern without being seen.

Time passed, and she began to feel sleepy, but at

last, her betrayer staggered out of the tavern, drunk. He headed down a path into the woods.

She followed him silently until they were out of earshot of the village, then ran up behind him and slit his throat. Out of breath, she summoned Zarblerg.

"Mistress."

"Consume this traitor. Make it look like he was attacked by animals."

She watched the grisly work with morbid fascination.

"That's enough; leave some for the villagers to find. Did you learn if this man told anyone else about me in the village?"

"He did not mistress."

"Good. Let's go home now."

She was able to fall asleep quickly but woke with a start at dawn, having dreamed of being captured and thrown back into the Bedlam Institute.

"Zarblerg, go to where you disposed of the bodies and watch unseen. When the officers come to investigate, listen to what they say and report back to me. In the meantime, I have a homunculus to torture." She smiled to herself.

The homunculus was chained to a pillar in the cellar where it stood, motionless. Millicent, wearing a large white apron covering her from neck to toe, paced around it, examining the strange half-man, half-machine.

"Moons, you are ugly. Can you speak?"

"You have no authority to question me." The creature's voice was strange, human yet mechanical, devoid of emotion.

She took out her stiletto and stabbed it in the arm; it did not flinch.

"Did you feel that?"

"Destruction of Justice Ministry equipment is a felony."

She stuck out her tongue.

"How did they make you? You were dead, weren't you? Do you need to eat? It would be grand if I could find an easy way to kill you clockwork monsters. I'm sure fire would work, but it's messy. Decapitation also, I am sure. Do you need to be oiled? Do you rust?"

The creature stared blankly ahead, showing no sign of fear or other emotion.

An idea occurred to her, and feigning contrition, she said, "I am very sorry about what happened. I would like to turn myself in."

"Turning yourself in would be a wise action," it said in its flat, emotionless voice.

She smiled. So, they were stupid; she made a mental note, then made another one for Benedict to bring acid the next time he came.

"I'm not going to turn myself in, you

abomination. First, I'm going to cut off your arm and study it, then find a clever way to destroy you."

Grabbing an old saw, she began to cut the arm where the mechanical part was joined to flesh. It was difficult sawing through the metal, but then, to her surprise, there was flesh and blood just underneath the metal, although there was no blood, only a little bit of an oily yellow substance.

She put the limb on a table and began to examine it. She expected gears but instead saw that it was a normal human arm covered with metal to make it look mechanical.

"This is strange," she said to herself.

CHAPTER 52

The Justice vehicle was in a ditch by the side of the road, lying on its side. The driver was in a bush several yards from the wreck as if thrown; the other two bodies were inside.

As the sun rose, a wake of vultures circled above the wreck.

The morning passed with a few villagers and tradesmen passing by, staring at the scene but keeping a wide berth and hurrying past, the feasting vultures paying them no heed.

By midday, a Justice vehicle, larger than the one that visited the castle, rolled in and stopped. Four officers were present; one was clearly in charge. The vultures reluctantly flew off as he approached to survey the carnage.

"Very strange, their throats have been ripped out. There haven't been wolf attacks like this in years," the chief officer said.

"Maybe a lycanthrope?" answered his lieutenant.

"Perhaps. Where is the homunculus?"

"It may have chased after the wolves. They are

very persistent; when they are on the trail of an assailant, they will not deviate," said the lieutenant.

"The Tech Ministry has ways to track the foul creatures; if it is alive, it can tell us what happened."

CHAPTER 53

After examining the arm, Millicent stabbed it where its heart should be, but that had no effect.

"Do you have a mechanical heart, too?"

"Your punishment will be worse the longer you delay turning yourself in."

"Told you, not going to turn myself in, you metal turd."

"When they find me, your punishment will be harsher."

She adopted a sweet, sarcastic tone as she began to dissect the heart, "How will they find you, my love?"

"The Tech Ministry is able to track all of my kind."

She turned pale. "You're bluffing."

Her smirk faded. "You're not. You're too stupid to bluff."

"It is against regulations to lie."

"Zarblerg!"

"Mistress?"

"Rip off this creature's head," she blurted.

She had the demon load the creature into the rowboat, and they rowed down to a swifter part of the river, far enough from the castle to avoid suspicion, she hoped. Then, they dumped the head and body overboard.

"Hopefully, it floats far away; maybe the water will stop them from tracking it."

Returning to Rabe Hold, she remembered that Regina would arrive soon with provisions for her uncle, so she watched nervously from her window, pondering what she would tell her. She considered lying and saying that he fell but decided that her friend should know the truth and was dying to confide in someone anyway.

Regina could see immediately that something was wrong with Millicent's manner. The previous day's experience still shook her. "What's wrong, Millie?"

"Your uncle, he is dead."

"How?"

"Justice officers came to arrest me. Your uncle came out trying to protect me, and the homunculus murdered him."

Regina became palpably angry, an emotion she never saw in her friend before.

"The Justice Ministry! Those homunculi are unnatural; I have heard things about their cruelty."

She paced around, trying to contain her anger.

"How would you like to help me destroy them, all of them?"

"But how, just us two? Oh, not the Red Death?"

"No," she chuckled. "I have friends. Don't be afraid, Regina," she warned. He is my friend. Zarblerg."

As she said his name, Zarblerg appeared, and Regina took a few steps back but kept her composure.

"I see; when do we start?"

Millicent smiled wickedly and a pact was made.

CHAPTER 54

Millicent's plans to move back to the city were progressing nicely. In a few days, her new townhouse would be ready for her to move into.

She would take the identity of an orphaned daughter of a mid-level administrator. Her new name would be Claudette. Regina would come with her and pose as her servant as part of her plan.

Millicent began experimenting with the spell dampener device, activating it, then attempting to cast various spells and noting down the results. At first, it was very discouraging, as all the spells she attempted failed utterly. But then she tried casting spells before activating the device and out of its range. The illusion spells all were dispelled when they got within one hundred and ten feet. The distance, she reasoned, would depend on the dampener's size and power, so the larger ones would have much larger ranges.

Then she tried a spell called Demballa's Menticide, which allows the caster to take over the mind of a human or animal, control it, see through its eyes, smell with its nose, and hear through its ears.

She cast it out of the range of the device on one of the stray goats, then had the goat walk towards the device. To her delight, it did not affect the spell; she could walk the goat right next to the device and even touch it. Additionally, the goat did not take control of her body during the spell but was merely captive in its own mind. She was able to break the spell at will. To cast the spell, she only needed some of the creature's blood.

Gumarich entered Director Aldebrand's office and handed him a paper saying, "The report you requested, sir."

His brow furrowed as he read. "Have you read this, Gumarich?"

"No, sir."

"Inspector Quentin began looking for that murderous daughter of Lucian outside the city and now seems to have gotten himself killed along with another officer and a Tech Ministry man."

"Incredible. How?" said Gumarich.

"It says they were attacked by wolves or some other wild animals. The homunculus is missing, and attempts to track it have failed to find any sign of it, not the slightest cog."

"Preposterous."

"My thoughts as well. It seems that if we are to bring this girl to justice, I must become personally involved. Bring me all her files, everything."

"Sir," Gumarich said and left briskly.

The death of Quentin and his team was too suspicious to be a coincidence. Aldebrand studied a map of the area. There were the ruins of an abandoned castle and a small village near the scene of the killings. It was there he would start.

"Gumarich!" he shouted. "Assemble a squad of men and a few homunculi. Bring a magic dampener as well. We leave in an hour."

Three wagons carrying Aldebrand, Gumarich, twenty justice officers, and three homunculi rolled through the castle gate just past noon.

Without hesitation, he exited the vehicle and approached the door of Rabe Hall.

He knocked and waited a few seconds before trying to open the door; it was locked.

"Homunculus, break down this door. Men, separate into squads and search the castle."

They rushed into the keep and quickly dispersed, searching every room.

When an officer opened the door to the library, there was a blast, and his charred body was blown against the wall, and the room burst into flames.

"Be careful; there are traps," Aldebrand shouted to his men.

"No one is here, sir, but people were living here very recently."

"She was here; the trap proves it. Search for evidence; bring me any papers you find." Aldebrand commanded.

CHAPTER 55

Millicent was spending a lovely morning relaxing in the courtyard, listening to the birds singing and reading a book titled "Brother Theodore's Guide to Immolation – 50 Spells for Vitiating Your Enemies", when she heard the dull ringing of the ghostly bells of her security wards. She ran up to the top level of the keep and through the window saw a force of some twenty men approaching, justice officers by their look. She cast a hawk eye spell and could see the man in the lead; it was Aldebrand. Her heartbeat quickened, her face reddened, and her hands tingled with hatred, but it was too many men to fight, and they no doubt had a spell dampener that would block her from using any magic and dispel any illusions she could cast.

The rowboat was ready at the dock, and she had a bag already prepared containing gold, a change of clothes, and her most important books. This moment was prepared for. Running into the library, she quickly stuffed her notebooks into a bag and prepared a spell that would be triggered when the door opened. It broke her heart to destroy the library, but she couldn't let the Justice Ministry find her books and papers, although she realized they would likely still deduce it was her.

She rushed down to the dock. The men had already entered the castle walls, and she had only seconds to spare. As the men rushed into the castle, she paddled out into the river and cast an illusion spell to make her boat look like a group of ducks from afar. She hoped the spell dampener didn't have the range to reveal her boat.

"Zarblerg."

He popped into the boat, causing it to suddenly pitch, and she was tossed back into the demon's belly.

"Damn it, Zarblerg, you are getting fat!"

"Apologies Mistress."

"Never mind. Paddle for me; it's hard to paddle upstream. They finally found us." She gazed back at her castle wistfully. "I'll miss Rabe Hold, but it was time to start work anyway."

In a few hours, they were in the cities' dockyards. Millicent bade Zarblerg to disappear, and she put on the clothes of a humble fisher girl. She refrained from using magic to alter her appearance, wary of proximity to a spell-dampening machine, and hoped her years away had altered her appearance enough to fool any casual observers who knew her.

This was the first time she had seen the city in the daylight since her escape. Much had changed, but much was the same. There was even more smog than she remembered. She spotted a few buildings with giant smokestacks, spewing dark gray smoke into the air. These were the new electric generators that somehow used coal and steam to create the electricity that was being wired into the city. In some of the streets, gas lights were replaced by electric ones. She hated their harsh white light. Some of the more wealthy homes had electricity put in along with electric lights, and moons only knew what other kinds of machines. Ugly scaffolding was being built above one of the main streets in the city, upon which a new train track was to be laid. Many of the factories had been converted to use electricity instead of steam power. Wires were being strung across the city like ugly spiderwebs. She could feel the power surging through them and despised the way they made her feel impotent magically.

She walked to Benedict's quarters, occasionally passing a justice officer or homunculus, but none paid her heed.

Benedict took her to the estate he purchased for her. It was a fine estate, although smaller than most of the other mansions on the street.

"It is adequate. Now go to Regina and bring her here," she commanded Benedict.

Millicent and Regina lived quietly for a time. They made due just by themselves; Millicent didn't trust anyone enough to hire as a servant. Regina loved the luxurious bed and huge kitchen but missed the serenity of the forest. There was a small courtyard with a garden where she spent most of her time. They spent long evenings in the parlor discussing Millicent's plan. Regina was hesitant, thinking it was far too violent, and she encouraged her to think of a better way.

CHAPTER 56

Millicent was on her own, strolling the streets, which she found helped her to think.

She saw a poster on a wall announcing a recital by Farinelli the Castrati. Memories flooded back to her of her time with her aunt, the concert they saw together, her meeting the maestro, and seeing him in the whorehouse and his betrayal of her. Anger burned in her heart, and she decided at that moment that it was time to get revenge on the singer.

She hurried to the theater, arriving just as the concert had begun. She sat in the back, in disguise, alternating between enjoying the music and anticipating the revenge to come. He delivered an exceptional performance, and the crowd showered him with adoration. But she remained unmoved, her heart still ablaze with hatred. After he went backstage, she left quietly and headed for the maestro's palazzo, remembering the address from seeing it on the card he gave her so long ago.

The abode was a large building set apart from the others in a fashionable part of town. She climbed over the wall and onto the grounds. The doors in the courtyard were locked, but she spotted an open window on the second floor. A drainpipe served as a means to climb up, and she emerged into his chambers. The house was utterly still and quiet; there were no servants awake. There, in his bedroom, she waited in the dark patiently, seated on a comfortable couch.

It was several hours before he returned home.

She heard the door open and one set of footsteps echoing on the stairway below. Finally, he entered the chamber and lit one of the gas lamps by the door.

He walked the long bed-chamber to his bed and then spotted her, sitting motionless on the couch.

He seemed unfazed and smiled at her charmingly. Perhaps strange women breaking into his home were common.

"Did Alessandro send you?"

She did not answer.

"How did you get in?" He turned to his open window. "Ah, very ingenious of you. I am very tired, but your ingenuity should be rewarded. Come." He held out his hand.

Millicent got up and took a step toward him.

"Do you remember me, maestro?"

He scrutinized her for a moment, "Forgive me, I have many fans; have we met?"

"Indeed. It was about four years ago. My aunt took me backstage to see you; you gave me your card and told me to visit any time." She walked around the room, looking at the paintings and statues.

"Again, I apologize; that sounds like a hundred other nights."

"You are forgiven; I have changed a lot since then. My hair used to be blonde."

"What is your name?"

She paused and walked toward him for a few steps before adding, "We met a second time in the Parlor of Lucinda the Red."

His smile faded, but she could tell he still didn't make the connection.

"Perhaps if you told me your name."

Millicent turned to face him directly, and her voice became harsher. "You saw me there, and informed on me to the Justice Ministry. Tell me, how much did they pay you?"

The change in his face was dramatic as his smile turned into a grimace, the color drained from his face, and his eyes widened.

"I am Millicent of the House of Ravens," she added.

"I did not inform on you, I swear!"

"I don't believe you; there was no one else who could have recognized me."

"Please. What do you intend to do?"

"I want to see if you will sing any better if I take

other pieces of you off." She drew her stiletto and took a step toward him.

He ran for the door, but she caught him and tripped him.

From the floor, he tried to scramble away and make for the stairway.

She caught him there and slashed him deeply in the belly with the stiletto.

He hovered for a moment at the top of the stairs, then tumbled down all sixty steps in a most dramatic way worthy of any opera, and by the time he reached the bottom, he was dead.

She was satisfied but not satiated; there was much more work to do.

CHAPTER 57

Garbed in pretty dresses, Millicent and Regina strolled arm in arm down the street by their estate and to the nearby park. She enjoyed showing Regina her old haunts and made Regina laugh hysterically when she told her about taking Zarblerg to the park.

On a wall near their house, they saw a poster.

"Galvanism! The new Truth. Tech Miracles! The dead will walk! Exposition this evening at dusk. Tower of Records Lecture Hall."

As disgusted as she was by anything tech, Millicent's curiosity was piqued, and she felt she had to attend, if only to learn more about her enemies.

"Tonight. We should go," she said to Regina.

"Will you be able to refrain yourself from murdering someone?"

"I'll be good, I promise."

They both laughed and walked on.

The lecture hall was a large square with a raised stage and tiered seating, much like a theater but not as lavish, simple, and stark as the typical Ministry of Records austere style. Millicent and Regina were early. Most of the five hundred or so seats were open, but people were filing in quickly. Sitting in the back they watched the crowd like birds on a wire. Most were well-dressed, upper-caste people, but there were some of the working class. Soon, the room was packed and noisy, with people chattering excitedly. No one seemed to know what was about to happen, but everyone was curious.

The lights dimmed, and a tall, hawk-nosed man walked onto the stage. It was Minister Tranton of the Tech Ministry, one of the men who murdered her father. Her body went stiff and burned with hatred. Regina touched her arm comfortingly.

He began speaking, "Distinguished citizens of Rathberg. Tonight, we will speak of the future. You have all no doubt been seeing many wondrous changes throughout the city as of late. You are also aware of the recent discovery of Galvanism and some of its miracles; the electric lights banishing the darkness with celestial radiance, the factories pulsating with the rhythmic heartbeat of machines, tirelessly crafting the dawn of a new era. Our streets are now safe again thanks to the diligent patrols of our homunculi justice officers, who never tire and are incorruptible. But these things only scratch the surface of what Galvanism makes possible. No longer need we depend on the fickle nature of magic or summon foul demons, for Galvanism is itself a force of nature, and cannot be stopped no more than we can stop a storm. It is superior in every way."

There were some mumblings in the crowd. Those magically inclined looked to their partner disapprovingly.

"We at the Tech Ministry have been working tirelessly, experimenting, and finding new uses for this miraculous force. Observe." He motioned with his hand behind him, and two assistants rolled out a man lying face down on a gurney.

"This unfortunate has injured his back grievously and can barely walk. But with a treatment of electricity, we can help him. Proceed."

One of the assistants produced some kind of paddle connected to a wire leading off into the dark backstage. He then placed the paddle on the man's back and nodded to someone off-stage, and a slight crackling could be heard. Millicent felt the electricity drain magic from her, making her lightheaded. She turned to Regina and saw that she also looked unwell. The man twitched slightly, and the paddle was removed after a moment.

"Now, Citizen Thonus, how do you feel?"

"Fine, your honor," the man answered.

"Now, get up and walk. It's okay, don't be afraid."

The attendants helped him off the gurney, and he stood on his own. He smiled and looked at the Minister.

"Go on," the Minister encouraged.

He took a few tentative steps, then turned and

began walking as well as any man without a limp.

People in the audience gasped, then began clapping.

Millicent looked at Regina and rolled her eyes.

"I am cured! Thank you, Minister."

The Minister smiled, and the man was led off.

"This is only the beginning, my fellow citizens. You see, we have discovered that Galvanism is the force behind life!"

Some in the audience gasped.

"Yes, you see, Galvanism is the life force itself!"

People began chattering, incredulous.

"It is true, and I can prove it."

He motioned to backstage again.

Another man was wheeled out in another gurney, but this time was completely covered with a sheet. The sheet was removed, revealing a man who was pale and rigid with death.

"This unfortunate was found, not an hour ago, floating in the river, drowned. As you can see, he is quite dead, his lungs not breathing, his heart not beating. Are there any physicians in the audience? Raise your hand, please. You, sir, please come up to the stage."

He pointed to a man in the audience, and he was ushered up some stairs to the stage.

The Minister handed the man an instrument

shaped like a horn. "Please check for a heartbeat."

The physician placed one end of the instrument on the man's chest and the other on his ear, listened briefly, then arose and shook his head.

"Thank you. Now, let us begin."

An assistant walked onto the stage with two paddles this time.

"This time, we will use more power."

The assistant placed the paddles on the man's chest, then a crackling could be heard, and the man's back spasmed, his back arching several inches off the table. The crowd gasped.

"Again," Tranton commanded.

Again, the paddles were placed, and the man spasmed.

The dead man began coughing and moaning and turned to his side, vomiting up some water. The crowd exclaimed in shock. He opened his eyes slightly and tried to look up. Millicent thought the eyes looked dead, like the homunculi. The crowd was in an uproar.

"Take him away; he needs time to recover."

The man was wheeled away accompanied by the physician.

Speaking loudly over the commotion of the crowd, Tranton continued, "Behold the power of Galvanism! Very soon, the dam will be finished and will provide the entire city of Rathberg with limitless power. Forsake your moon worship and magic spells; Galvanism is the one true divinity. Thank you."

He bowed and walked off stage.

The audience stood up and cheered, chattering excitedly among themselves.

Assistants remaining on the stage began handing out pins with a design that looked like a yellow lightning bolt in a circle of black, the new emblem of the Tech Ministry. The audience eagerly took them and pinned them to their coats. Millicent was fuming and half considered summoning Zarblerg to tear the people to pieces.

"That man may have been breathing, but he was not alive," Regina said to Millicent.

Millicent answered, "I think that is how they make the homunculi. The mechanical parts on them are just a disguise, to make people think they are mechanical, and not just dead people walking."

Millicent and Regina looked at each other gravely and left.

CHAPTER 58

Regina went to bed, but Millicent was too upset, so she went out into the city to roam like she used to in her youth before everything happened. She wore her black outfit, hid her hair under a hat, and headed for the rougher parts of the city, taking her trusty stiletto.

For hours, Millicent prowled the city, just walking, talking to no one, and reminiscing.

By now, she was in the neighborhood known as The Shambles. Here, the miracles of Galvanism were not appreciated. She noticed some graffiti scrawled on one of the buildings.

"To hell with the Clockworks."

Further on, the symbol of Galvanism that had been painted on a wall was roughly painted over with black, and "Galvanism be damned" was written below. Next to that was a drawing of a penis.

The beginnings of an idea sparked in her mind.

She passed by a rowdy pub named The Drunken Tabby and, on a whim, went inside.

The room was crowded with rough-looking

men; she felt down around her belt, confirming her stiletto was there. A fight was in progress involving several patrons while others cheered them on; the rest of the bar ignored the fight. She made her way to a quieter part of the room, trying to be inconspicuous and observe and listen. Unfortunately, she couldn't make out much of the conversation due to the room being so loud, so she ordered a beer and sat down at one of the long tables. The conversation was mainly men jesting with other men, mostly in the theme of playfully questioning each other's manhood, and got tiresome quickly. She didn't like these people as much as those in the village. She was about to stand and go when someone mentioned a homunculus killing an innocent woman on the street, and she blurted out, "Fuck the Tech Ministry."

The man closest to her turned and looked as if he just noticed her. "Aye, lad, you sound like Lud."

"Who?"

"The man over there with the silver hair." He pointed at the next table to a tall man with silver hair.

When the man turned away, she quietly got up and sat across from this Lud. He was in the midst of a conversation with a group of men who were listening to him intently. She could tell he was respected by how they all listened to him.

"I tell you, lads, if things keep going as they are,

there will be no jobs left for us workers. We'll all be replaced by machines or them clockwork monsters."

She listened for a time, then left quietly, smiling, her mind churning with plans.

CHAPTER 59

In the morning, at breakfast, she spoke to Regina. "I have been thinking about what you said about my plan being too violent, and I think I have a better one. The workers all hate the Tech Ministry. Their jobs are being replaced by machines, and people are being killed by the electricity and the factory engines. I think with just a little nudge, they will rebel against the Tech Ministry, and I won't have to put my original plan into action."

Regina smiled, "Brilliant! However evil the Tech Ministry is, it's not worth laying waste to the entire city to destroy them."

Millicent nodded in agreement.

The next evening, she returned to The Drunken Tabby after first casting a spell of beguiling to increase her persuasiveness. There, she found Lud sitting at a table quietly. She ordered two drinks and sat down next to him.

He gave a suspicious sidelong glance but took the drink, "Thank you, lad."

"I heard what you said about the Tech Ministry

last night. I think you are right," she said.

"Do you now, lad, or should I say, lass?"

He was intelligent and observant, that was good. She decided to take the direct approach.

"The Tech Ministry killed my father and I hate them as much as you. I think many people feel as we do, and with the right leader, we can force the ministers to stop what's happening."

"Bah, without money and influence, nothing can change in this city."

"I have money and influence."

"Now, why should I trust a little poppet like you?"

Millicent was beginning to get a little annoyed at his disrespect and was about to let fly with an insult, but she was interrupted when a man staggered into her, knocking her hat off and exposing her long hair.

"Sorry." As he looked back at her, he noticed she was a woman. "Well, sorry, I am indeed; why don't you let me buy you a beer?" His speech was extremely slurred, and he touched her shoulder far too familiarly. Already annoyed, this was enough to set her into a rage. Quick as a snake, she twisted his arm and slammed it down, breaking the wrist in the process. He screamed in pain and rage. "You little bitch!"

He tried to grab her with his other hand, but she ducked, and he fell into another man. This was enough to spark a brawl, with several men getting involved in the fighting and her trapped in the middle. By this time, she had enough and cast a flash spell, causing a blinding light to burst from her palm for a fraction of a second, just long enough to blind everyone in the room momentarily and allow her to slip out quickly.

She returned home, angry but not defeated, resolving to try again.

CHAPTER 60

The next evening, she decided to take a different approach. She cast an illusion spell, taking the guise of a tall man in wealthy clothing. The pub was in a section of town that was not electrified, and she was confident the spell would not fail. She also brought Benedict as her bodyguard; a wealthy man would be expected to have a bodyguard, and she didn't want anyone to attempt to rob her, as her mission was to speak to this Lud person again.

"What do you want me to do exactly?" Benedict asked as they walked to the pub.

"Just stay with me and not say anything; I don't expect any trouble."

"I must say, seeing you as a man is very jarring," he said as they entered the Drunken Tabby.

The patrons of the pub stared as they entered, but dirty, confrontational looks by Benedict made them quickly look away. She bought them drinks and once again brought one to Lud, who was at the same table as usual.

At first, he just looked and ignored the drink she

had placed before him.

She spoke—with a strong male voice this time. "It was my niece who spoke to you last night."

"It was not I that offended her-" Lud said, holding his hands up.

"I know, but we decided it best for me to come instead; you see, I have interests in seeing the Tech Ministry fail. And my niece and I agree that you are the man who can organize and lead the people into a revolt against them."

Led looked at her, sizing her up. "Such a thing requires capital."

She took out a sack of coins and placed it on the table before him.

"So, you are serious?"

"Deadly serious."

Lud picked up the bag and felt its weight. "Alright, I'll be this leader. Got nothing much to lose."

"Excellent. We need a name for this group... I know, Luddites!"

"Suits me."

"You begin recruiting more like-minded men. I will return in a few days," Millicent said.

She handed him the necklace of a raven made out of a dark silver material. "Here, wear this; it will give you good luck." She had bought it during the day from a shop, and it was magically charmed to give the wearer charisma.

CHAPTER 61

The following day, with the help of Regina, they brainstormed some slogans, had them printed up on a flier, and paid some urchins to nail them up across town.

LUDDITES!
Rise Up Against the Tyranny of the Clockworks!

and

The Justice Ministry are Necromancers!

They also purchased ads in the paper with similar wording, including an article that was written as an expose.

"Homunculi are the Walking Dead." read the headline.

"Reliable sources have confirmed that these homunculi abominations are actually the dead that have been resurrected by the Tech Ministry back to a grotesque simulacrum of life using the Galvanist Necromantic magic. These unfortunates are used as slaves by the Justice Ministry. Forcing them to do atrocities against the citizens that even the justice officers would not dare to commit."

CHAPTER 62

After a week, Millicent returned to The Drunken Tabby in the guise of the wealthy man. The place had a buzz about it.

Lud was standing, addressing the entire room. She watched for a while, pleased.

He took a break, and she went to him, and they shook hands.

"Our numbers have grown; your adverts have done well," he said.

"Yes, I can see that," she replied.

"However, we are beginning to attract the attention of the Justice Ministry. They came to our demonstration in front of the factory and beat us up."

"Here, use this to bribe the officers to turn their attention elsewhere." She handed him a sack of gold.

"And what of the homunculi? They cannot be bribed."

"Don't worry, I will take care of them. Keep growing the group; we still need more men. Find some deputies to help spread the word."

CHAPTER 63

Millicent was dressed as a boy and had a clever disguise on her nose made of wax, a false beard, and a mustache on her face. She would be near the Justice Tower and didn't want to take any chances. After surveilling for a time, she noticed all the homunculi coming and going from the same building, a plain windowless building adjacent to the Justice Tower. As she walked by, she could tell a spell dampener was in use, but this didn't discourage her. She waited until dark and saw a man leave the building, making sure he was in plain clothes and not an officer. Then she followed the man past the center of town and waited until they were alone on the street. She cast a beguile spell on him, a simple enough spell she could complete in this section of town with fewer electrical lines, and commanded him to walk, guiding him to an empty warehouse she had rented in The Shambles, where there was no dampening. The warehouse was empty except for two chairs arranged side by side. She sat the man on one chair and cast a sleep spell on him, then took out a vial and her stiletto and collected some of his blood from his arm, being careful to not make a fatal wound. Finally, she bandaged his wound.

"Zarbleg. After I complete my spell, I will take command of his body; my body will remain here asleep. Guard me until I return."

She cast the Demballa's Menticide spell, and suddenly, she was looking through the eyes of the guard.

"Okay, Zar, release me. Guard my body until I return," she said in the voice of the man.

She looked at her own body, it was a very strange experience. Seeing a stray straw on her hair, she gently removed it.

She hurried back to the building with the homunculi. A couple of homunculi guards at the door paid her no heed due to the badge she was wearing.

There was a vast room filled with cots but without mattresses, blankets, or pillows; the monsters apparently didn't care much for comfort. Many of the cots contained homunculi; most of the creatures were off duty at this late hour. The room was utterly silent, as the creatures didn't snore.

Another man emerged from a door. There was a moment of panic, then she quickly remembered she belonged here.

He walked closer, looking puzzled, "What are you still doing here, Claus?"

"I forgot something."

"Oh, well, see you in the morning."

With relief, she watched the man leave the building and go into the room where the man had come from. There was a gigantic metal vat against the wall with a spigot. Turning it, a foul-smelling liquid came out. Then she noticed some large bowls, ladles, and a number of smaller bowls neatly stacked up on tables. This was their mess hall, so they did need to eat. She guessed they would line up here in the morning and be served the swill from these vats. Looking up at the ladder attached to the vat, she smiled; she had a plan.

Quickly, and quietly she snuck out of the building without incident and returned back to the warehouse.

She canceled the spell and instantly was back in her body, then she turned to look at the man, seeing him with a terrified look on his face staring at Zarblerg, who stared back at him.

"Zar, kill and consume him."

The man screamed.

When it was over, she asked the demon, "Tell me when the homunculi feed."

"At sunrise, mistress."

"How often do they feed per day?"

"Once."

"Do they always have the same thing, the swill

from the vat?"

"Yes, Mistress."

"Wonderful! This will be easy," she said, grinning.

When she returned home, she rushed into the kitchen where Regina was cooking and breathlessly blurted out, "I have a plan to kill the homunculi! We can poison them, they all eat together, we can get them all at once. We need something extremely concentrated but enough to kill two hundred homunculi, and it needs at least twenty minutes to take effect to ensure they all take it before they start to keel over and get suspicious."

With raised eyebrows, Regina held up her spoon and said, "Slow down. They are not human; we don't know if a poison will kill them or what dosage."

Millicent paused momentarily and said, "Then let us conduct an experiment and try the potion out on one."

Regina stirred the pot for a few moments, thinking. "Alright, I will need to go to the country for the ingredients."

"No need, I know a place that has everything."

"Very well, we will need Belladonna, Oleander leaves, wormwood, and honey."

"Honey?" Millicent questioned.

"To counteract the bitterness."

Millicent laughed, "Of course. You get the honey; I'll get the rest."

CHAPTER 64

Millicent stepped into the apothecary and stood there momentarily, the sights and scents bringing back fond memories. Hieronymus was behind the counter, reading a paper. His hair was a little more white, but otherwise, everything in the shop was as she remembered. She had taken the precaution of casting an illusion spell to alter the appearance of her face, fearing he would remember her and alert the authorities.

"May I help you?" he asked, showing no sign of recognition.

"Yes, I will need 6 ounces of oleander leaves, 3 ounces of belladonna berries, and 2 ounces of wormwood. Please."

His eyebrows raised in surprise, but he said only, "Certainly, miss."

She watched as he gathered the reagents, reminiscing about her youth spent in the shop and enjoying the familiar smells.

Hieronymus placed the items in small bags and said, "That will be fifteen ducats."

She paid him and turned to leave.

"Your manners have improved, Millicent," he said as she walked away.

She hesitated for a moment but did not turn, surprised.

"Your appearance is well disguised, but mind your voice. Whatever you are planning, count on my support. If this Galvanism nonsense continues, I will lose my shop," he added.

She turned her head and gave him a smile, then continued out the door.

Regina took the ingredients to the kitchen and made a venomous concoction, boiling them for hours until the entire potion could fit into a small bottle. Millicent was there the entire time but had fallen asleep. Regina woke her and told her it was finished.

She squealed in delight and hugged Regina.

"Be careful. You shouldn't need the whole bottle. Try half and then give more if it doesn't work."

CHAPTER 65

Millicent waited for an hour before she saw her prey.

A solitary homunculus was patrolling one of the streets near the harlot district. She crossed the street and approached it. When she got close, she slashed it in the chest with her stiletto.

"Take that mother fucker!" she sneered and ran off.

"Halt! You are under arrest for attacking a justice officer."

She ran, but not going so fast that it would lose her. She led it to a large sewer pipe, made sure it saw her enter, and was following. Watching it enter the dark tunnel without hesitation, fear, or attempts at stealth, she continued leading it on until they were in the catacombs. She came to a dark nook and hid.

When it was close, she summoned Zarblerg and said, "Grab it!"

Zarblerg grabbed the unsuspecting creature and held on with strong hands.

"Unhand me, I am an officer of the law," it said.

"Shut the fuck up. Bring it."

She led Zarblerg to Aldous' old lair, which she had prepared in advance.

"Put it in the irons."

Zarblerg fastened iron cuffs around its wrists and ankles, the ends of which were bolted into the wall.

"You will be severely punished for the kidnapping of a justice officer; I advise you to release me."

"Eat shit," she said as she took out the vial of cloudy liquid.

"Now, drink this."

She put the vial to the creature's lips and tried to get it to drink, but it kept its mouth closed.

"What is the punishment for kidnapping a justice officer?"

"Ten years in a labor camp minimum."

When it opened its mouth, she managed to pour a good amount down its throat, spilling the rest on its face.

"That should do it; now we wait and hope our moons are in phase. Zar, keep watch and come to me if you see any justice cucuzzas coming."

Impatiently, she watched the creature, waiting for any sign of the poison taking effect, using a timepiece to keep track of the time.

"How do you feel, cucuzza?" she asked after twenty minutes.

"There is a burning sensation in my abdomen. I believe I need medical assistance."

She grinned and jumped up and down with joy.

"Please, summon aid," it said, with what seemed like just a trace of emotion.

"Ha, now it begs!"

It began foaming at the mouth and convulsing, and in sixty seconds, it sagged down against its chains, unmoving. Millicent kicked at it to be sure it was dead, then gave a whoop of joy.

"Zarblerg! It worked, let's go."

CHAPTER 66

The next day, she returned to the apothecary, not bothering with a disguise this time. Heironomous was more than happy to provide her with more ingredients.

Regina got back to work brewing more of the poison.

By evening, everything was ready, and she repeated her stalking of a worker, following him, luring him to the warehouse, and bespelling him, with Zarblerg guarding her body. She walked back to the Homunculi barracks with a bottle containing enough poison to kill half the city. The power she felt made her giddy.

Like the last time, the guards let her in without a word. The mess hall was deserted, so she climbed up the ladder of the vat and poured in the poison. But it suddenly occurred to her that it should be stirred. She looked around and saw a gigantic paddle, like one used for boats, but its use was clearly for stirring. She was glad her body was strong because she could barely move the paddle through the thick liquid, but after some time, she was satisfied that the poison had been mixed in thoroughly.

Now, all that remained was to wait until dawn, when the feeding would begin. She had to ensure it worked and couldn't pass up watching the spectacle. She sat behind the vat, nearly nodding off a few times, but finally, the time arrived.

A man entered the mess hall, and she walked around to greet him.

"Ah, thank the moons you are here. Claus still hasn't reported. Hope he is alright. Don't just stand there; get to filling the barrel."

A large barrel on wheels was nearby. She pushed it over to the spigot and began filling it. Next, she wheeled it back to a table where the man was waiting. He began to ladle the slop into individual bowls for the monsters to take.

"Don't just stand there, you idiot! Help me. It's almost feeding time," the man said.

Millicent found another ladle and began helping him.

He looked over and said, "Not so much; these monsters hardly need anything. As far as I'm concerned, they are dead."

She continued with her work, and the other man did the same. Soon, the long table was filled with the small bowls containing the poisoned slop.

A loud buzzing alarm caused her to jump. The other man laughed at her reaction.

In a few seconds, the homunculi began filing in, each taking a bowl, drinking the concoction all at once, and then placing the empty bowl into another large barrel. The process was very smooth and orderly, eerily mechanical.

"Well, go on, start taking the bowls to the washroom."

She took the barrel and wheeled an empty one over to take its place. She rolled it out of the kitchen and down the hallway where she assumed the washroom was. Not bothering to do any actual washing, she kept impatiently looking through the door back into the barracks. Some of the creatures had already left, but some were there taking orders from a human officer who appeared sometime during the feeding. By now, all the homunculi had fed. Impatiently, she looked at her watch; things should have begun happening any moment now.

There was a crash, and she saw off to the side that one of the monsters had fallen to the ground, writhing in pain and foaming at the mouth. Then another, and another.

She watched for a time, immensely enjoying the mayhem as more and more homunculi fell down, dying. Human officers poured in. Fun time was over; it was time to break the spell.

She returned to the kitchen, climbed up the ladder to the vat, and jumped in, breaking the spell immediately before the body hit the liquid and drowned. Overjoyed, she returned to her home to give Regina the news.

CHAPTER 67

The homunculi were gone, but Millicent felt they needed some kind of spark to reach the next phase of her plan. Without telling Regina, she left the house in the dead of night. She went to one of the buildings that housed a power plant that generates the electric power. She picked the lock to the back door and crept inside. The machinery was very loud, but she saw no workers. She knew the general principle behind the machine. The kettle was heated by coal, and steam was created. The steam would travel up the pipes and turn the pistons, which in turn would somehow generate the electricity; that part was a mystery to her.

She also knew that an explosion would occur if steam could not escape. She climbed up the machinery. The ladder was attached to the giant kettle and was very hot, but fortunately, she was wearing gloves. Atop the ladder was a metal wheel, which she deduced would close the valve that released the steam. She began turning it. It was hard to turn and took a dozen revolutions until it stopped. The steam was shut off, and the piston stopped turning. There was an eerie stillness.

She didn't know how long it would take for the explosion to happen, so she hurried back down the ladder. A worker had come to investigate, saw her, and shouted at her. She leaped down on him from the ladder, causing him to collapse hard against the floor. Then she cut him with her stiletto. She heard another shout but didn't dare dally. She ran out of the building the way she came and kept running. After she was a block away with another building between her and the power plant, she felt safe. That is when the explosion happened. It was the loudest sound she ever heard, and her ears rang. After a few moments of silence, she heard screaming and shouting. She rushed home and went to bed, but it took hours for her heart to slow enough for her to sleep.

CHAPTER 68

Late the next morning, Millicent went to the dining room and found Regina reading the paper. When she entered, Regina read aloud.

"Galvanist Power Station Explodes! 35 innocent's dead. A tragic accident occurred at the power station on Green Street. A powerful explosion completely destroyed the building and several other buildings in the block. The blast broke windows up to a mile away. At least 30 people were killed instantly, and five more in the fires that ensued. The Tech Ministry claims it was sabotage but can provide no evidence to support the claim."

Regina looked at Millicent, "You wouldn't happen to know anything about that, would you?"

"How terrible, those machines can be dangerous," Millicent said as she munched on a cream bun. Regina watched her for a few moments, then put the paper down and left, obviously upset.

Millicent felt it was time for the Luddites to take their cause to the general public and had fliers printed up.

LUDDITES!

Gather at the south docks on the night of the double half-moons

Join us

TO PUT DOWN ALL MACHINERY HARMFUL TO COMMONALITY

She met with Lud, as the old man, and they spoke about the meeting that would happen in three days.

CHAPTER 69

The dam appeared like a tremendous curved wall, on one side holding back the millions of gallons of water in the newly formed lake and on the dry side rising up like an enormous man-made cliff. Below the cliff was a mostly dry riverbed flowing into the city below. The Tech Ministry ordered the coal factories to be closed today, and the view to the city a mile away was clear.

The grand opening celebration began early in the day, and the Tech Ministry spared no expense. A 20-piece band played gay music atop a raised dais. The crowd was in the thousands, mainly from the upper crust of Rathberg. The women wore their most colorful hats, and the children held whirligigs, handed out free by the Tech Ministry by the hundreds for the occasion. There were boat races in the new lake, which was formed upriver to the dam.

No one glanced at the stooped old man, wearing an old-fashioned, slightly dusty black suit and over-sized black top hat. A pretty young redhead accompanied him, his daughter, it could be assumed. Regina was enjoying the spectacle, eating fried balls of dough purchased from one of the many vendors, but Millicent, hot in the black suit and hat, watching everything like a predatory cat, had only one thing on her mind; how to destroy the dam. The structure was impressive; it would not be easy to destroy.

CHAPTER 70

As dusk approached, Minister Tranton took the dais and began making speeches. He boasted about the outstanding achievement of the structure and its difficulty of construction. Then, he attempted to explain how the dam worked to create electricity, emphasizing that it was technology and no magic was involved, but the crowd didn't care.

A drunk man began shouting obscenities, and quickly, two men from the crowd, justice officers in plain clothes no doubt, started beating him, then dragging the unconscious man off.

Tranton paid no heed. After finishing his speech, he threw a bottle of wine, smashing it against the dry wall of the dam.

"Now, citizens, as the sun sets, we see our great city below us falling into darkness. But the time of magic and darkness is over; now is the time for technology and light. Open the gates!" Tranton shouted.

Millicent strained to see someone atop a tower on the dam turning a valve. After a few moments, water began rushing out of the multiple holes at the lower part of the dam, at first slowly, then in a great torrent.

"Now activate the generator." he shouted.

Out of sight a switch was activated by a technician.

Electric lights strung out across the area flickered to life, causing people to blink in the harsh brightness. Millicent felt all of the magic drain from her instantly, causing her to almost faint, but Regina held her arm until she recovered.

"Now, citizens, watch the city below," Tranton shouted triumphantly.

After a few seconds, the lights in the city began to flicker to life.

The crowd gave a great cheer. It was a glorious day for Rathberg, but Millicent fumed with evil thoughts.

She was confident she could temporarily stop the generator by turning the valve that controlled the water. There would be guards, but those she could handle. The problem was that more guards would come and simply start the generator up again. She needed a way to destroy the dam permanently. She went through all the spells in her repertoire, but nothing had the power to destroy such a large structure, at least not quickly, which was a requirement.

CHAPTER 71

Millicent went into the apothecary to see Hieronymus and ask for his advice.

"I want to destroy the dam, but I have no suitable spells. Can you help me?"

His eyebrows raised in surprise. "Destroy the dam, yes, that would be difficult. But it would be a very effective blow against the Tech Ministry."

He thought for a moment. "I have no potions or compounds to destroy such a huge structure. But there may be a way."

He came out from behind his counter and walked to the back of the store, Millicent following. She noticed he was smaller and more stooped than she remembered; he must be ancient now.

They came to a shelf, and Heironomous bent down to move some sacks out of the way. Behind them was a loose board, which he removed, revealing a hidden compartment. He reached in and pulled out a book. It was extremely dusty, and he blew on it, causing a great cloud of dust to go into Millicent's face. She had a fit of coughing, which became a fit of laughter as she appreciated the jest, even though it seemed accidental.

"This is the Spell-book of Albralex. It is the only known copy." He caressed the binding lovingly. "It was to be my retirement emolument, but now, with magic all but banned...I am happy to contribute it to the cause," He handed the book over to Millicent.

"Thank you, but how can it destroy the dam, Heironomous?"

"I have no magic talent myself, but I remember seeing one of the spells was called Ten Thousand Elephants. It will cause the earth to quake with such power that it could destroy a castle or a dam."

Her eyes lit up, "Thank you, Heironomous, it is perfect."

CHAPTER 72

Dressed all in black, Millicent scrambled over the wall at Rathberg Zoo. She had gone there often as a child; it was one of her favorite places in Rathberg. The place was quiet late at night, although she could hear a low rumbling sound; the lions. The giant cats were her favorite; they were beautiful and deadly. Then she heard footsteps and stepped into a shadow until the guard passed. She remembered where the elephants were and headed that way. An owl, perched at the top of his cage, stared at her with bright eyes. She contemplated freeing it but decided she didn't have time. The elephants were out of sight, inside some enclosures. She leaped over the wall and quietly crept into the elephant enclosure. One giant beast was there; its eyes were closed, and it was asleep. Casting a sleep spell on the animal to ensure it didn't wake, she took some of its blood and put it in a vial.

Vial pocketed, she went back to where she jumped in, only then realizing that it was too high for her to jump on this side of the wall, the enclosure being on a lower level. She stood there feeling stupid, then got an idea. She went back to the elephant and reversed the sleep spell, then cast an enchantment spell on the beast and had it crouch down so she could climb on top. Next, she commanded it to stand and walk over to the wall. Carefully standing up on the giant beast, she could just reach the rim of the wall with a short jump and scramble up and over. She waved thanks to the elephant and quickly returned home.

CHAPTER 73

The Ten Thousand Elephants was the most difficult and elaborate spell she had ever seen. It required a full day of preparation and many different reagents, including some dirt from a fresh grave and the elephant blood.

The spell involved casting it into a crystal, which, when broken, would release the spell. This would mean she could release the spell quickly and be gone, which was fortunate because her plan required meticulous timing.

She acquired the rest of the materials from Heironomous and locked herself in the study. It took a full day and night, but finally, she had the spell contained in a crystal the size of a robin's egg. With only a little more work, she was able to cast it into a second crystal, a backup in case the first was not powerful enough. All that was required was to throw it on the ground to break it and release the spell. Finally finished, she fell asleep on the floor in exhaustion.

CHAPTER 74

The night of the double half moons soon came, and she resolved to appear as herself instead of her male alter ego. She dressed all in black in a simple outfit a worker would wear on their day off, although made from much finer material and perfectly tailored, of course. Regina insisted on coming and was dressed simply as an ordinary female factory worker.

The crowds were already thick a few blocks away from the docks. Making their way through the crowd was slow and difficult. People were converging in the warehouse where the meeting would be. The crowd hummed excitedly as they pushed their way inside; the building was already full. The warehouse was empty of goods except for a group of crates positioned in the center where some men stood. Another man, tall with white hair, Lud himself, emerged atop the makeshift stage, and the crowd cheered.

"Citizens of Rathberg! Friends! The Tech Ministry continues to install their machines in our factories, putting honest and skilled men out of work, producing inferior goods that only benefit the profit of the factory owners. Their homunculus abominations walk our streets, terrifying our women and children. The harsh glare of their electric lights blind us and scare the wyverns away. Their foul machines chewing up the fingers and limbs of its operators - mostly children, what's more. Electric wires everywhere, deadly to the touch. How many people do you know have been killed in such a way?"

Many in the crowd shouted in the affirmative.

"Our beautiful city now blemished by iron scaffolding for their trains. Our proud traditions of magic vanishing by decree, driven out by the electric generators, their noise keeping us from sleeping.

Just last week was a train crash that killed dozens. Skilled weavers thrown out on the street with not even an hour's notice, replaced by young children who are forced to work 18 hours a day. Miners are out of work because of their foul digging machines. Washers out of work and those that remain sickened by the chemicals spewing out of the gigantic vats. Iron workers with lungs blackened by soot from stoking the coal-eating beasts. And now the explosion on Green Street!"

There were shouts of anger from the crowd.

"This must not stand. Let us march forth to the Tech Ministry and make them acknowledge us."

The crowd erupted into such a raucous cheer

that the roof rattled and began to move, pushing Millicent and Regina along with it. The throng of people, thousands strong, marched to the Tech Ministry Tower. The crowd was joyous, and spontaneous songs and chants were being sung.

The Tech Ministry tower came into view, and the crowd fanned out, surrounding it. Unlike the ancient towers of the other ministries, this building was new. It was less tall, only ten stories, but broader, and the design was blockier and constructed of plain cement bricks.

Most of the windows were dark, and the workers, no doubt, were home for the night. People were shouting slogans, some threw rocks at the building, and windows began to break.

Then, a commotion arose from behind her. People shouted that homunculi were attacking. Impossible! She destroyed them. Unless... A horrible thought occurred to her. Was it possible they were brought back to life by electricity as they were originally? She climbed up the back of a dismayed tall man like a squirrel so she could see over the crowd. There was a large force of homunculi and justice officers marching in a line, cutting down people with swords. The man wrenched her off, and she fell.

There was screaming, and the crowd began to flee. She became separated from Regina, the force of the crowd pulling them apart like a mighty ocean wave.

Panic began to ensue, and she was being crushed by the crowd. She was having difficulty breathing and tried casting a levitation spell, but it failed, dampened by the proximity to the tower. She was moving with the throng, being pushed along with her feet, and not even touching the ground.

Just when she was beginning to black out, the pressure subsided, and she found herself a few blocks away, having been carried without even walking. She had to see what was happening; she needed to get above the crowd! A building had a door broken into by the mob, and she entered. She went up some stairs, and a man rushed by her, stealing a crate of something. Continuing to the top floor, she emerged onto the roof. Below and a few blocks away, she could see the mayhem. The line of homunculi was forcing the crowd away from the Tech tower. There was an enormous group of them, hundreds easily, probably most of the homunculi in the city. Many people were lying on the ground in pools of blood. Regina was down there; she had to find her.

In the thick of it was Minister Morcant. When he heard of the riot, he rushed to the scene, wanting to partake in the glory of squashing the protest himself. By then, the rioters had already been routed, but he took command immediately and began issuing orders, "All homunculi, form up in front of me. These rebels must be put down. Kill all you can."

As they were being driven off, he shouted, "Drive

them to the Shambles. Block off any side exits. We will take this opportunity to destroy their nest as well. By the end of the night, these Luddite scum will be eradicated."

The homunculi swept their way past her building, so she ran down and doubled back to the carnage, looking for Regina. Hundreds of people were down, dead or dying. After a few minutes of searching, she found her friend lying against the wall of the tower. Blood was oozing from her nose and mouth, and her eyes were open, staring lifelessly. Millicent found herself sobbing, her chest contracting in sobs beyond her conscious control, tears freely flowing. She couldn't remember the last time she cried, and the sensation was bewildering. After a few minutes, she was able to regain control and sit down against the wall. Soon, rage took the place of grief.

She rose and seized a sword from the lifeless grasp of a fallen homunculus, her eyes ablaze with blind rage. She ran ahead to the line of justice officers. They were pushing the rioters away, killing any that got close enough. From behind, she swiftly dispatched one, then two, then another, and yet another until she reached the other rioters.

By now, the troops had noticed her behind them and had begun to surround her, en masse. Instincts for survival overcame her blood lust, and she dropped her sword and turned to run with the rest of the rioters. It was a complete rout, with the rioters fleeing for their lives. Many rioters managed to escape in the chaos but many were killed by the troops bearing down on them, and a cluster Millicent was in was being channeled away from the Tech Tower.

Now, they were in Ambrus Square, in the midst of The Shambles. It was a wide square that was used as an open-air market during the day. Clusters of Justice officers blocked all the exits, and the main force of homunculi was bearing down. They were trapped.

Only a few dozen rioters were left alive with her. The enforcers shouted for them to surrender, and those with weapons dropped them. But Millicent only smiled. She knew they had made an error, driving them to the section of the city free of any spell dampeners, and they had cornered the most powerful magic user in the city.

All she needed was a few seconds to prepare. She started an incantation, feeling her skin tingle with magic, smelling the odor of petrichor in the air, then glowing with magical energy as she moved with the spell and chanted words of power. She finished, and there was a moment of stillness, of silent expectation, as if a dam were about to break. Then waves of energy burst forth in a circle around her, spreading out with the speed of sound. In two heartbeats, it was over. All was still except for cries of pain and anguish. The homunculi in front took the brunt of the spell. Very little was left of them except some stains on the ground and walls enclosing the square. Officers further away were torn apart, leaving piles of limbs and body parts. Unfortunately, the rioters that were trapped with her were also destroyed, but at the moment, she didn't care. A few human officers along the periphery were alive, some injured, some not. Exhausted by her powerful spell, she summoned Zarblerg and bade him finish off the rest.

She went through the bodies, looking for Morcant, hoping he was still alive. There was a cluster of men still alive behind the homunculi. One by one, she finished them off and then recognized Morcant. His leg was destroyed and covered with blood, and he was dragging himself along the ground with his arms, making pathetic noises. She crouched down in front of him.

"Minister Morcant, do you remember me? You know, the fifteen-year-old girl you kidnapped and tortured, the one whose father you murdered, the one you sent off to be abused in a madhouse."

Eyes wide with animal terror, he stared up at her and tried to speak but instead made awful croaking noises.

She sat down on the ground in the lotus position, not minding that it was slick with blood, and studied him for a few moments.

"You?!" he exclaimed, now recognizing her.

"Yes, you remember, don't you? You called me

harmless then. Do you still think me harmless?"

He shook his head.

"After I kill you, I will destroy the Justice and Tech Ministries and restore the Magic Ministry to its former glory," she said in a sing-song as if she were speaking to a toddler.

"No, please-" he croaked.

With that, she lifted his head up by the hair and slowly cut his neck with her stiletto, watching his blood drain slowly away.

Zarblerg came up beside her, breaking her reverie, "Mistress, it is finished."

She looked around. He had done his duty well, and the streets were still and silent. Wyverns were already arriving to feed on the carrion.

She stood up and said, "Well done, Zar, you may go."

Now alone, with adrenaline subsiding and numbness beginning to settle in, the events of the night were finally taking their toll. Regina was dead, and this victory did nothing to stem the ache she felt in her heart. She wandered the street exhausted, and in a daze, eventually finding herself at The Drunken Tabby. Inside were only a handful of men, all pale, downcast, silent, defeated; some had blood on their clothing.

Spotting Lud, she sat down next to him. As he turned to look at her, she was shocked by his haunted, blank stare and ghostly pale face drawn into a grimace. The hand holding his cup was shaking noticeably.

Putting her hand on his shoulder gently, she said, "Lud, we have won; the homunculi and most of the justice officers in the city are dead."

He stared at her for a moment and said, "Won? Everyone is dead. My comrades. They massacred us. This wasn't the plan." He looked down and began to weep.

She turned away and ignored him. He was broken but no longer needed. But he was right— they hadn't won, not yet. The Tech and Justice Ministries were still intact, and her revenge was not yet complete.

She drank deeply from her cup and quietly said to herself, "You are right, Lud. This is only the beginning. When I am finished, the city will bathe in blood. The Tech Ministry will be completely destroyed, and magic will be restored to its rightful place."

Her mind wandered, and she had a vision of Regina lying dead in the street, alone, her body being picked at by wyverns. She ran all the way back to the Tech Ministry tower. There were now some people wandering through the dead, looking for loved ones, some sitting by the bodies, mourning. There were no justice officers in sight. Luckily, the wyvern had not yet begun to feed on Regina. She stayed by her side for a while, eventually drifting into a troubled sleep.

CHAPTER 75

Millicent woke the following day. Many people were around with carts, taking the bodies away. She paid one to take her friend home, where she laid her down on her bed to await burial.

Once home, she eagerly fetched the newspapers from the front steps. To her dismay, the Justice Ministry suppressed the true story of the riot.

Last night's events were framed as the Justice Ministry putting down a disturbance by a rabble of anarchists, and Minister Morcant was killed bravely defending the city. Aldebrand was sworn in as the new acting Minister of Justice. The officers and homunculi slaughtered in Ambrus Square were not even mentioned.

She entered the street, expecting things to feel different, but nothing had changed. She even saw some Justice officers on patrol, as if nothing had happened. The area by the Tech Ministry tower had been cleared of the dead. The only indication of last night's riot was some blood stains on the cobblestones.

She made arrangements for Regina to be buried,

purchasing a large headstone and a fine plot in Ridgeview Cemetery, where the most important people in Rathberg were buried.

On the way home from the cemetery, Millicent passed by High Street, strolling and window shopping. A filthy beggar with no legs was perched on a stool against a wall by the Haberdashery shop.

He grabbed for her as she passed. "Spare a coin mistress?"

Instinctively, she drew her stiletto but held her strike, sensing no danger.

"Millicent?" the beggar whispered.

She stared for a moment, and then suddenly, recognition came to her. It was Cerberus, her long time butler! The once proud guard looked a shadow of who he once was; his legs were gone, his hair was now long and pale gray, he had rags for clothing, and he was filthy.

"Cerberus," she whispered back, shocked and dismayed by his appearance. "I thought you were dead."

"I was as close as can be. Only some powerful healing magic was able to save my life, but not my legs. They only saved me so they could question me. They wanted to know about some magic crystal the master had hidden, but I didn't know. Not that I would have told them. They asked me about you too, where you could be hiding. But I told the fiends nothing. After I healed up, they just tossed me out into the street." His voice was hoarse and weak. The state of him broke Millicent's heart.

"What happened that night?"

"I was about to lock up for the night when a dozen Justice enforcers rushed into the building. They tried to arrest me but I fought back with my sword, killed a couple of them, but they were too many. My legs were cut to shreds. I saw them run up to your apartment before I blacked out. Thank the moons you were gone. When I woke my legs were gone. Minister Morcant himself interrogated me, but I told him nothing. I was locked up in Nightstone for a few months with the rest of the Magic Ministry people but after I healed, they knew I was no threat to them so they released me out here in the streets to beg like a dog." He began coughing.

"You have been a loyal friend, Cerberus. You will stay in my estate until we can find you a good place to stay."

This incident served as a catalyst for enacting the next phase of the plan. She would free the prisoners of Nightstone, and they would serve as her army.

CHAPTER 76

Disguising herself as a beggar, she watched the prison from the street, studying it. It was different in design from the Bedlam Institute, more fortress-like, and secure. It was in the city proper surrounded by a tall wall, the building had almost no windows, just a few narrow slits up high. Supplies came in once a day, but was well guarded and searched.

The prison was formidable, but she knew it must have some flaw.

Disguising herself as an old woman in Ministry of Records garb, Millicent visited the Hall of Records. No one looked at her, and she was allowed to peruse the maps library freely.

To her disappointment, plans for the prison were unavailable, so she took the most detailed maps of the city she could find, which showed the general location of the prison.

Back in her office, she stooped over the map, studying it carefully. Suddenly, she grinned widely. The prison was formidable, but had a weakness; it was built above a section of the catacombs.

Work on the tunnel began immediately. Using every bit of her trigonometry tutoring and some refreshment from her books, she found the closest part of the catacombs, calculated the angle at which to construct the tunnel, and put Zarblerg to work digging.

Cerberus, now in a wheelchair and dressed in fine clothing, answered the door and admitted Benedict.

"She will see you in the office," he said.

Sitting behind her desk strewn with maps, notebooks, and papers, she said to him, "Part of my plan involves freeing the Magic Ministry people who have been imprisoned in the Nightstone Detention Center. I plan to use the catacombs to tunnel underneath and free them all at once but I need someone inside to feed me information and organize the men."

"Wait!" He held up a hand and his face started to redden. "Are you about to ask me to get myself imprisoned in Nightstone?"

"Yes. I need someone inside to warn the men that they will be freed and create a distraction in case the digging gets too loud."

He glared at her, "You expect me to do this?"

"Not for very long, only a couple of weeks at most."

"A couple of... No, I have done everything you asked for all these years, but this is too much. I know I betrayed you, and I'm sorry, I didn't know they would treat you like they did, but I paid back my debt many-fold."

Her old self would have gotten angry and threatened him, but she resolved to be more measured and calculated in her thinking. "Yes, you have done much for me and I am grateful, but I have also made you wealthy."

"Well, hardly wealthy."

She sat back in her chair. "Very well, do this one last thing for me and I will release you from your obligations to me. And I will pay you ten thousand ducats."

"After I escape, I will be a wanted man."

"Ten thousand ducats is enough to let you live like a king anywhere you like, beyond the city." She considered mentioning that Rathberg would be all but destroyed anyway when she was finished, but decided against it, sensing he would not approve.

"Twenty."

She leaned back in the desk chair, then said, "Very well, twenty thousand, but I will not pay you in full until all of this is finished."

"And what if you do not survive."

"If I don't I will take the entire city with me," she said, smiling.

He looked down, considering, "Alright, I will do this one last thing for you, and then I will never have to see you or your demon ever again."

This last remark hurt her somewhat. After all they had been through, she assumed they were comrades and thought their sparring was more playful than anything, but she hid her feelings and said, "Deal."

CHAPTER 77

Millicent and Benedict sat outside a cafe adjacent to the Clockwork Spire's main entrance and watched while sipping tea. Millicent was disguised as an older woman with a matronly dress. She looked like she could be Benedict's mother. It was the middle of the day, and the street was crowded with people bustling around.

"Who is this man I am about to murder?" Benedict asked, scanning the crowd.

"Gumarich. A justice ministry man, second in command to Aldebrand, one of the men that murdered my father and put me in the madhouse."

"I see. I can make him die slowly if you prefer."

Millicent was genuinely touched, "No, that will not be necessary. There!" she exclaimed, "that one with the beard and brown hair."

Benedict rose, stepped onto the sidewalk, and pretended to accidentally bump into the man.

"You cur!" Benedict shouted at him.

"I beg your pardon, but you bumped into me," Gumarich answered.

"How dare you call me a liar!" Benedict drew his rapier.

A woman in the crowd screamed. Others cleared the way, trying to avoid the altercation.

"I am unarmed. I have no blade." There was just a trace of fear in Gumarich's voice.

Millicent watched from her table, sipping her tea, enormously entertained.

"Take mine." Benedict tossed him the rapier and drew a dagger from his boot.

The fight began. Gumarich was no novice, nor was he an expert swordsman like Benedict. His strategy looked to be that he would stay on defense and hold off Benedict until justice officers arrived, having no idea of his opponent's skill. Benedict circled him, throwing an occasional thrust, testing his skill and gauging his opponent.

Millicent heard the shrill whistle the street justice officers carried.

"Kill him, damn it," Millicent whispered to herself.

She saw the uniforms through the crowd, approaching fast.

Benedict did as well and went for the kill stroke. He feinted the sword and struck Gumarich in the heart. He died in seconds. Three justice officers burst through the crowd with swords drawn. Benedict dropped his weapon and raised his hands like he was surrendering, but then began moving them in the air, in a way that Millicent taught him, to make them think he was trying to cast a spell.

One shouted, "He's a mage!" Then three officers tackled him and put his hands in manacles behind his back and led him away.

Millicent wanted to cheer and clap her hands but was wise enough not to bring attention to herself, so she quietly slipped away instead. "Sorry Director Aldebrand, your assistant was killed in a senseless street fight." she whispered to herself as she walked away from the commotion, giggling.

CHAPTER 78

Work on the tunnel had progressed nicely; Zarblerg worked as fast as ten men.

While she waited for the tunnel to be complete, she worked on other aspects of her plan.

Preparing a large chamber at the end of the tunnel to use as a garrison and storehouse, and purchasing food, clothing, cots, weapons, and some reagents needed for spells. She also discovered that the spell dampeners had no effect below ground.

The tunnel was now very close to the surface. The tricky part will be to find the optimum section of the prison to break into.

It was night-time. Millicent, in the disguise of a beggar, carried a caged rat to a dark alley near the prison. She cast Demballa's Menticide on the rat. Being inside the mind of the rat was claustrophobic, the creature's intelligence being so primitive. Zarblerg guarded her body while she guided the rat to the prison walls. As a rat she was able to scale the wall easily and enter the grounds. Inside she found a courtyard made of broken concrete and some wispy weeds. The place was dismal indeed. Passing by a bit of moldy bread she had to fight the urge to nibble on it. She began circling the building looking for a way in and found that she could climb up the walls easily due to the coarse texture of the veneer. She climbed up and entered by one of the narrow windows.

She beheld a huge square chamber with cells along the perimeter, in two levels, their doors facing the center. In the center was a small guard room with bars along each wall allowing the guard to observe every prisoner's cell simultaneously. Two guards were in the guard room, but they appeared to be asleep, as did everyone in the cells. She scrambled down to the main floor of the prison and felt a low vibration through her sensitive paws coming from below. The main goal was to find the spell dampener, so she looked for the way down into the lower chambers.

There were two doors in the corner of the room without bars. Fortunately, there was a space large enough under the doors for her to fit under. She peeked into the first door. It led down a corridor to another locked door. Past that was a room with tables. Sitting there were several other guards. She doubled back to the cells and took the second door, leading down a flight of stairs.

She found herself in another hallway. The damp, musty, crypt-like odor was overpowering to her sensitive rodent nose. At the end of the hallway was a door, from which the humming sound was coming. She squeezed under the door and saw the spell dampener machinery, looking just like the one in Bedlam. Satisfied, the next order of business was to find a good place to emerge from the tunnel. There were several store rooms, one of which had a thick layer of dust on the floor, indicating it hadn't been used in years. It was ideal.

Next, she needed to find Benedict before dawn when the prison would begin to rise. Tediously she went from cell to cell. After about twenty cells, she found him. He was sound asleep, so she bit him in the toe. He sat up violently, cursing, and was about to whack her with a book when he seemed to awaken fully and say, "Oh it's you, it's about time."

In her condition, she could not speak, but she prepared a little note ahead of time and tied it around her neck, which she presented to him.

After opening it, he said, "Moons, I can't read this; it's too dark, and the lettering is too small."

No matter, he can read it in the morning, thought Millicent.

The note read, "Tomorrow night, after midnight, tell everyone you trust to be ready."

She bit him again, just for fun, then canceled the spell and returned back to her body.

Back in her body, the memory of being a rat made her qualmish. She felt dirty and desperately wanted a bath, but there was no time.

Using the rough map that she had, and her memory of the prison's layout, she guided Zar's tunneling to hopefully find the correct spot.

After a few hours, they reached some roots, and she knew they were near the surface. Using a hand drill, she drilled a hole upward until it broke through. Then she inserted a spyglass she had specially made, allowing her to see through the hole. They were inside the prison walls but in the courtyard. The building was about ten feet away, and the store room would be another ten feet in that corner.

She ordered Zarblerg to dig twenty feet further.

Just a few hours before midnight, they reached the spot. Then began digging vertically but quickly struck concrete.

"It must be the floor of the building; use the drill to make a hole," she told Zarblerg.

It was tedious drilling through the concrete, but an hour before midnight, they broke through, and she repeated the procedure with the spyglass.

She saw a darkened room with a thick layer of dust coating the floor, confirming her suspicions that this was likely a storage room tucked away in the cellar. Millicent instructed Zarblerg to expand the aperture quietly, mindful of the need to avoid attracting unwanted attention.

After an hour, a hole was big enough for a man to fit through. She lit a lantern, raised a ladder up through the hole, and climbed. A spider web grazed her face as she emerged from the hole. She cursed silently, hating spider webs on her face. She called for Zarblerg to join her in the room, crept into the hallway and to the door leading to the spell dampener. In a few minutes she had the lock picked and they were inside. Not wanting the thing to explode in her face like last time, she began pulling at wires. With one last pull the machine died, and the humming was gone.

She raced up the stairs, and opened the door to the chamber of cells.

This time, there were three guards in the middle guard chamber. She would have to use a quick spell to disable them before they raised the alarm, so she cast a quick lighting spell that fried all the guards at once. One however, managed to raise the alarm before he died.

Another contingent of guards ran into the chamber. Zarblerg intercepted the surprised guards and attacked. Fortunately, the entrance was small enough that only one or two guards could attack him at once.

After she ran to the guard room she realized her mistake. The keys were on the hip of one of the dead guards, out of reach. The prison lock was formidable, big and strong, and would take too long to pick. Looking over she saw that Zarblerg was able to fight the guards off and prevent them from coming in. Instead she cast a telekinesis spell. It was difficult because she had just cast a powerful lightning spell, the keys were heavy but after a few moments they were in her hands.

By now, Zarblerg had killed all the guards, and there was a lull, but she knew many more guards would be coming.

She ran to the cells and opened them as quickly as possible, not taking the time to speak to anyone but going from door to door. When she reached Benedict, she instructed him to lead the men down to the tunnel while Zarblerg watched for more guards.

"Start leading the men down into the tunnel. It's in the cellar, in one of the store rooms. The door is open."

She heard a shout of alarm. More guards were coming, and there were still more doors to open. The quiet order was replaced by pandemonium with the guards trying to get in, Zarblerg fighting, and bewildered prisoners shouting out in dismay. She handed the keys to one of the prisoners and told him to open the rest of the doors while she grabbed a discarded sword and helped Zarblerg to fight off the guards. The last of the prisoners were gone.

"Zar, let's go!" she yelled, and they ran down to the tunnel. The door to the cellar had a lock, but it would not hold the guards for long. After everyone was safely in the catacombs, she ordered Zarblerg to collapse the tunnel.

The authorities would take time to discover how the prisoners escaped, organize a party to enter the catacombs and begin the search. They would be safe here for a time.

Her mind was racing with the next steps to her elaborate plans when Benedict approached.

"I'm free to go now, right?"

"Huh? Oh, yes. Thank you for everything," she said distractedly.

"Can I have some money? I need some debauchery to cleanse me of the stench of the prison."

She handed him a sack of coins.

"You will get the rest when this is all over," she said.

She looked around at the escapees. Many of them appeared elderly, and some looked frail, yet she recognized the potent magic they wielded and knew that many among them harbored demons.

She climbed atop a crate and shouted, "Gentlemen!"

Most in the crowd did not notice and kept chatting, bewildered and shocked about the whole situation.

"Gentlemen!" she shouted again, louder.

One of the older magicians who was nearby looked at her haughtily and said, "Who is this poppet of a girl addressing us?"

She kicked, sending him sprawling backward with a bloody nose.

The crowd took notice and quieted.

"Now, Gentlemen. I was asked who I was. I am Millicent of the House of Ravens, daughter of Director Lucian, and your savior."

She paused for effect as the men stared at her bewildered.

"I have broken you out of the prison in order to set things right. Together, we will avenge all those killed in the coup, take back the Ministry, and restore magic to its rightful place in Rathberg!"

The astonishment felt by the crowd was palpable.

"How can a handful of us old men win against the Tech and Justice ministries combined?" one man shouted.

"Have you forgotten your power? You are the most powerful magicians in Rathberg!" Millicent answered.

"Their foul machines dampen our magic," one mage said.

"They will be destroyed," Millicent said.

"Yes, and they have an army of homunculi," another mage cried.

She answered, "No, they do not, because I killed the homunculi, every last one of them, along with a good number of officers. And do not forget we have our demons. Zarblerg!" for effect Zarblerg materialized there beside her.

There was an excited murmuring.

"I have been planning for this since the coup, and I also have magic."

"Magic indeed," someone scoffed.

There is a spell well-known to all magic users. It has no practical use, but it is helpful in demonstrating magical ability. It is used by the Magic Ministry to grade novice spell casters and by experienced ones to show off their strength. She cast the spell, and the air became charged with energy, causing hair on the back of necks to rise. Instantly, an aura of crackling energy surrounded her, and she hovered in the air. The color and brightness of the aura indicated the power of the magician. She glowed orange-red, the most powerful color, and was bright enough to hurt the eyes of those close to her and light up the far corners of the cavern like it was daytime. Her display was the most powerful anyone in the room had ever seen.

Awed, the room was silent.

"Now be quiet, and let me explain my plan..."

When she finished, the room remained quiet for a moment, and men began speaking.

"I want to restore the Magic Ministry, but I want no part of this mad plan," a tall old man said.

"I concur. We should form a committee and plan a more suitable plan," another said.

"Does anyone else feel that way? I promise you

will not be punished," Millicent said.

Several other men murmured agreement.

"Those who do not want to take part in taking back the city from the Tech Ministry, you may return to the prison." she motioned to the tunnel where they first entered, not mentioning that it was now collapsed.

"You can't send us back there!"

"Why not? I released you from prison, and I can put you back. These men murdered my father, and I will show them no mercy. If you don't have the heart to do what must be done, stay out of my way."

"I agree with Lady Millicent; these Galvanist fiends are destroying our way of life and must be stopped at all costs!" one of the men said.

The men that were hesitant seemed to reconsider, no one tried to leave.

"It is your right to not participate, but I will not have you interfere. If you attempt to hinder me in any way, I will destroy you. You may stay here, you will be safe and fed well."

The hesitant mages nodded meekly.

"Those of you who want to help, come and tell me your discipline and show me your demon if you have one," commanded Millicent.

First up was a mage of about sixty with long gray hair who bowed to her and said, "My lady. I am Balthazar. I was second in command to your father in the Ministry, who I admired deeply."

"Thank you, Balthazar. What disciplines did you study?"

"Conjuration."

"Excellent. You will be of great help. Show me your demon," she said.

The mage nodded, and a man-sized, green humanoid creature with a hideous lacertilian face and spikes all over its body appeared.

"What is your name?"

It hesitated.

"Tell her," he commanded.

"Albramonethsah," it said, its tongue flicking in and out as it spoke.

"Right, I'll just call you Al. Next!"

A slender magician with a thin black mustache named Phineas summoned his demon, who, from all angles, looked like an ordinary pigeon.

She looked at the pigeon, and then the mage with her eyebrows raised, "Does it have any powers?"

Phineas smiled and nodded at the bird. Its eyes glowed red, and suddenly, Millicent felt her body overcome with pain, and she collapsed to the ground. The mage nodded again, and in another instant, she was completely back to normal, and the bird had normal black eyes again.

She got back up, impressed but not angry. "Okay,

that teaches me to not judge a demon by its appearance. Can it do that to a group or just one person at a time?"

"One at a time, but it can kill; it was very gentle with you."

"I love it," she said as she stood up, "What is it called?"

"Shedim."

A tall mage of about 50 was next.

"My name is Severin, my lady, and I am honored to help you in any way I can in your endeavor to destroy the Tech Ministry." He spoke with a charming aristocratic accent. "My discipline is Abjuration."

His demon resembled an ordinary young woman with dark skin but had red eyes. Its face was a bit too angular, and the eyes were far too cruel to be ordinary human eyes. Millicent thought her attractive and made a note to imitate her look someday with makeup.

"Interesting, what can she do?"

"If I give her a knife and unleash her, everyone in this room will be dead in ten seconds."

It smiled evilly.

"Oh, I like her. What is she called?"

"Lamashtu."

A short, fat, bald magician was next. "Lady Millicent, I am called Malthus. I am very pleased to meet you and grateful for breaking us out of the prison. My discipline was Abjuration, spells of protection, and such."

"Good, let's see your demon."

What appeared was a creature with features so alien and hideous that Millicent grimaced and looked away. "Okay, you can make it go now."

After it disappeared, she composed herself and asked, "What can it do besides make people throw up by looking at it?"

"Asgoth can paralyze an enemy and quickly devour it."

"Fun. Next!"

Only ten of the mages had demons of any power, but it was more than enough for her plans.

They had dug a second tunnel which emerged in an alley quite near her estate. She led the ten mages through and they all entered the estate through the servant's entrance. The rest of the mages remained in the cavern, waiting for her instructions.

A lavish feast was prepared in advance and spread out along the long dining room table.

The mages sampled the food eagerly, no doubt sick of the prison food.

"Your magic is impressive, Millicent. Lucian taught you well, and he would have been proud," Balthazar mumbled with a mouth full of chicken.

"But you said you had no magic tutor the past

four years? Who taught you The Art?" Severin asked.

"No one, but I had some good books," Millicent replied.

"What discipline did you study?" asked Severin.

"All of them."

"Indeed," he said, eyebrows raised. "But not Necromancy, I assume?"

"Of course not." A trace of a naughty smile showed on her lips.

They spoke into the night. Millicent enjoyed being able to speak to others about magic, and it reminded her of the long talks she used to have with her father.

CHAPTER 79

Millicent gazed up at the sky. The sun had just set, and Mitra had risen over the skyline, full and glorious, bright enough to read by. Petra was just starting to peek over the skyline to the east, and she was also full.

It was the night of the double full moon and the night of the one hundred and twenty-fifth Moons Masquerade Gala. It also was the night she chose to enact her vengeance. This night would bear witness to her drama of revenge, and Ophidian Hall would be the theater of her vendetta.

The Twin Plenilune was Rathberg's most important holiday, and everyone was outside on the street, enjoying the bright moonlight. Even the smog respected the holiday and cleared to allow good viewing. Perhaps it was because the factories were shut down and coal was not being burned.

Millicent wore a fine black dress, which was fashionable but not outrageous like her first gala. This time, she did not want to stand out but fade into the background so she could observe unmolested. Although she could not resist wearing a raven mask, it was only fitting.

She sat out on her balcony, waiting until it was time to leave, watching the street. Many people were out, including families and children, all enjoying the moonlight that made the night almost as bright as day. There was music, games, food vendors, and entertainers. The excitement of the children was contagious. Some waved stick pennants of Petra and Mitra in the air and ran about gleefully. Some held balloons painted like anthropomorphized versions of the moons. Later, the drunks would dominate, but now, early in the evening, it was a safe and wholesome celebration.

She went to her drawing room and inspected her small army of mages. They were dressed plainly in black as servants, with hats and scarves, their demons hidden, of course.

To avoid attracting too much attention, they were instructed to divide into three groups and to keep a distance from each other on the short walk to Ophidian Tower.

They arrived at the hall from the rear and went to the servant's entrance. Millicent picked the lock, and they entered quietly. Inside, there were some servants frantically preparing the food and drink for the banquet, but they were quickly subdued non-violently and locked in a store room. The rest of the servants were already in the hall. The mages took the servant's masks and wore them. As one servant left the hall to bring an empty tray to the kitchen or remove some trash, they were grabbed by the conspirators and replaced.

Most of the servants were now replaced by her mages, and Millicent stepped into the banquet hall.

The gala was much like she remembered it from not so many years ago, although it seemed like another lifetime. She walked to a quiet corner and observed.

As she might have expected, due to the purge, there weren't many Magic Ministry people, just Minister Ambrosius, some low-level administrators, and those willing to submit to the authority of the Tech Ministry. She spotted Technician Cynebald among a clutch of tech people.

But where was Aldebrand? Ah, there, surrounded by a gaggle of fawning women.

She didn't see Tranton and began to worry, it was imperative he was here, but it was still early.

A middle-aged bald man spotted her and approached. He said something, but Millicent feigned a coughing fit until he gave up and walked away.

There was a commotion near the entrance way, and she saw Tranton arrive with an entourage. The crowd spontaneously began clapping. This display of supplication annoyed Millicent.

Now, everyone was here, and it was time to begin the entertainment.

She left the building and hailed a cab. Anticipation was building in her breast. The streetlights were now on, as the moons were beginning to sink lower in the sky.

She had the cab drop her off a few hundred yards below the dam, and ordered him to wait, promising a generous tip. Then she went the rest of the way on foot, keeping off to the side of the road out of sight. At this time of night, the road was deserted, and she saw no one.

At the dam, she saw only three guards and almost laughed out loud at the carelessness. Such was their arrogance that they thought no one would want to harm their precious dam.

Hiding behind some boulders, she summoned Zarblerg. "Zar, I have an important task for you."

Carefully, she took out the crystal containing the Ten Thousand Elephants spell. It was wrapped in some soft felt padding.

"Take this crystal. And don't drop it!" She hissed. "In 30 minutes, I want you to materialize onto the damn, there," she pointed, "in the middle, just next to the building, and throw it down on the concrete. When it breaks the spell will be released, and you can go. Do not risk fighting the guards, just get out of there. Do you have all that?"

"I have some difficulty with measuring time, Mistress."

"Fanculo! Alright, then see Mitra up there," she

pointed to the moon rising just above the treeline, "When the moon goes behind the trees and you can no longer see it, that is when you should do what I said. Can you do that, Zar?"

"Yes Mistress."

"Don't let me down," she said as she left.

Millicent snuck back past the guards and ran to the waiting cab, telling him to return to Ophidian Tower. Leaving such an important task for the demon worried her greatly, but she couldn't afford to expend any energy fighting guards. She needed all of her stamina for what was to come next.

When she jumped out of the cab she could feel the ground trembling slightly. The spell was cast, but was it strong enough to destroy the dam? If not she would have to rush back and use the second spell crystal. She watched nervously, waiting for the streetlights to go out.

CHAPTER 80

When Zarblerg smashed the crystal, the spell was released and there began a slight shaking, but its strength doubled every second. First, cracks appeared in the cement on the face of the dam, followed by some loud, ominous fracturing sounds. Then, all at once, the dam crumbled, and a huge opening appeared with water rushing out, growing larger every second. The earth stopped quaking but it was too late for the dam. In a few seconds there was nothing left of the dam except some concrete on either side of the river.

Millions of tons of water rushed with incredible force through the opening and down the riverbed towards the city, tearing and crushing everything in its path. In the docks and the low-lying factory sections of town, flood water was tearing through buildings like sand castles and inundating the streets. Fortunately, those sections of town were mostly deserted due to the time of night and the holiday, which primarily celebrated in the center of town.

CHAPTER 81

There! At the edge of the city she saw the lights going out, the darkness moving rapidly towards her as the electrical power was killed. She hurried inside the building, wanting to see the reaction of the people in the hall.

She heard gasping and muffled panicked shouts from the hall. The moment she had dreamed of for years had finally come. She stripped off her bland uniform, revealing a scanty red dress underneath, and rushed into the main hall.

The lights going out were the cue for the mages to bar all the doors. Each took off their mask and summoned their demon, who stood beside them, awaiting instructions.

Not yet noticing this in the darkness of the hall, Minister Tranton addressed the crowd, "No need to worry, my friends. In a moment, the backup generators will start up, and we will be back in the light. The dam is new, and there are bound to be some outages."

After a few moments, a grim tension began to build among the revelers. The hall became silent in dreadful anticipation as it slowly dawned on the crowd that something was terribly wrong.

CHAPTER 82

Outside Ophidian Tower, the rest of Millicent's army sprang into action. Squads of mages waited outside the generator stations, waiting for their cue. When the lights went out in the city, they were to destroy the generators. Mages skilled in evocation commanded the wind to blow the doors open and then cast firestorm spells inside the buildings. So as to not burn the city down, they controlled the fire with wind and water magic so that the generator buildings were the only ones affected.

Another force of mages, skilled conjurers, created a giant golem and ordered it to break into their generator building and destroy the machines.

Just outside the main hall, in the entry hall, Lamashtu went to work on the guards who were coming to investigate. She moved so supernaturally fast that she was hard to see, like a blur. In a matter of seconds all the guards were dead and the floor was awash with blood.

CHAPTER 83

People began to panic and rush for the doors. Frantic hands clawed at door knobs, only to find them stubbornly locked, a grim barrier against their escape. Women screamed.

Millicent cast a spell, causing a glowing orb to form high up in the ceiling, illuminating the hall in a garish red light. The crowd quieted momentarily, thinking salvation was on hand, but then as they saw the mages without masks, and their demonic familiars surrounding them, there were screams of terror and gasps of shock.

Millicent climbed up on the stage, the confused musicians not stopping her, the screaming subsided.

"No, Minister Tranton, your electric lights will not return. People of Rathberg, you see, the dam has been destroyed, and the city is being flooded as we speak."

The crowd erupted into a cacophony of shouts, a curious mixture of fear and outrage.

"What?! Who are you?" Tranton shouted over

the din.

"Don't you remember, Minister? I am Millicent of the House of Ravens, daughter of Lucian; you remember him surely, the one you tortured and killed."

His mouth hung open in shock.

She turned to the musicians cowering behind her, "Let the orchestra go; they are blameless."

The doors creaked open, revealing a crimson scene of carnage in the long and wide entrance hall. Lamashtu stood there impassively, coated head to toe with blood, holding a knife still dripping, her face beaming with pride, much as an artist would when revealing their canvas. The bodies of two dozen or so guards littered the floor, strewn about haphazardly in a macabre scene of chaos and violence.

The musicians hesitated. She motioned at them with her hands, "Flee while you can, you fools, she will not harm you!"

The musicians ran, dodging the bodies, occasionally slipping on blood, and escaping into the night.

One of the men in the crowd who was not a musician tried to make a break for it and ran for the doors. Albramonethsah grabbed him and tore his throat out with its claws.

Women screamed.

"That was unwise. Now, most of you wives, as loathsome as you are, are guilty only by association. You may go," Millicent continued.

Their eyes shifted between Millicent and their husbands, uncertain, torn between loyalty and self-preservation.

"Shoo. Go! Farti friggere!" She said.

A few began a cautious retreat, soon joined by most of the rest and breaking into a run, their high heels clicking against the polished floor in a scene that reminded Millicent of a flock of chickens fleeing from a dog.

"Or stay if you please; it doesn't matter. The rest of you can stay for the ceremony; prizes will be awarded," she said cheerfully and smiled. She paused for a moment and commanded, "Seal the doors."

Lamashtu closed the doors, and Malthus cast a spell that caused them to fuse together, trapping everyone in except for the servant's entrance.

"Now, isn't this cozy? The cream of Rathberg, together in this one room." Millicent paced back and forth on the stage, enjoying herself.

There were about a hundred men left and a few wives. They were mostly members of the Justice and Tech Ministries, with a handful from the other ministries.

"You must be mad!" a man yelled.

"Mad meaning angry, yes, very much. Mad in the sense of crazy, well, perhaps. I was in Bedlam, after all."

"Now, let us begin the festivities. Our first prize is awarded to Minister Ambrosius. Congratulations. Please come here."

She spotted him in the crowd. He was trying to cower behind some other men.

"There, that one that looks like an ugly woman."

She pointed, and Albramonethsah grabbed him, then threw him down in front of Millicent.

"Minister Ambrosius. You are a disgrace to the Magic Ministry. You collaborated with the men who conducted the coup and betrayed my father, who was supposed to be your friend and comrade. You are a puppet of the Tech Ministry and a disgrace to the office of Minister. For this crime, I sentence you to be consumed by Asgoth."

The Minister screamed, and the crowd became mute in abject terror.

Asgoth sprang into action, paralyzing Ambrosius and moving toward him in its weird, uncanny, shambling way. Before Ambrosius could get up, the demon was on top of him, seeming to adhere to the Minister like a blanket of treacle, and despite his thrashing and twitching, the demon merged with him, quickly absorbing his flesh. In about twenty seconds, there was nothing left of the Minister.

Many in the crowd vomited, and some fainted.

Millicent felt a little queasy, too, but continued.

"I know that was gross, but believe me, he is getting off easy. Now, Technician Cynebald is next. I remembered your name because you are bald. Come on, don't be shy."

He, too, had to be grabbed by Lamashtu and thrown in front of Millicent.

"Now, baldy. You were the one that pulled the lever on the machine that tortured me-"

"I was just following the orders of Minister Tranton!" he screamed, his voice pitched high in abject terror.

"Yes, dear, I know. Trust me he will be getting a much worse punishment. Now, where was I? Yes, you pulled the lever on the machine that tortured me and killed my father."

A few people in the crowd murmured, not knowing the true details of the coup.

"That's right, he burned up right in front of me," she continued.

Cynebald tried to get up and run but Asgoth had him paralyzed, and he was only able to drool and twitch a little.

"For this crime, you will be given to Shedim to destroy."

The pigeon demon took off from its master's shoulder and landed in front of the director. Its eyes began glowing red. Cynebald froze, and his eyes began bulging. His face turned beet red, and after about ten seconds, his eyes burst out of his skull, and he slumped down dead.

"Gross!" she said, but she was grinning. "Well, now we are getting to the fun part! Lamashtu."

The dark-skinned demon grinned.

"Go in the fountain and do your thing."

"Albra-whatever, start grabbing people and bringing them to Lamashtu."

The lizard demon began grabbing people from the crowd and tossing them like grain sacks to Lamashtu, who quickly slit their throats, letting the blood drain into the fountain, then throwing the bodies away like discarded wine skins.

"Not him! I have something special in mind for Minister Tranton," Millicent shouted as Lamashtu grabbed the Minister. "And you, Aldebrand, I haven't forgotten you."

"You little witch, I knew we should have killed you with your father!" Aldebrand shouted.

"Yes, you should have," Millicent replied, grinning.

Terror gripped the men, their eyes wide with fear as adrenaline surged through their veins. In a desperate bid for survival, a handful of them, fueled by primal instincts, began a futile effort to fight back. The demons dispatched them quickly; Albramonethsah breaking their necks, Zarblerg tearing out their throats, Asgoth consuming them, and Shedim destroying their minds. Some of the trapped men cowered in the corners. Aldebrand and a handful of others stood their ground defiantly.

Soon, thick crimson fluid had replaced the sparkling pink wine that was formerly flowing through the fountain. After a few dozen bodies were emptied, the fountain began to overflow into pools of crimson on the marble floor.

"Okay, Lamashtu, that will do for now," Millicent commanded.

Millicent took out a sack of sulphur and began tracing a circle around the fountain.

Severin, now realizing what she was doing, stepped toward her, "Now see here, do you mean to summon a demon with that blood?"

Phineas chimed in, "The demon summoned by that much blood will be an arch demon; not even a pentacle could hold it."

"I know, and I don't intend to use a pentacle," Millicent answered without looking up, not pausing in her work.

"You must be mad; it could destroy half the city!" Malthus cried.

Lamashtu grinned.

"That's the plan, starting with this room," Millicent answered.

Balthazar spoke, "Lady Millicent, what you are

doing is extremely dangerous; I beg you to reconsider."

"Okay," she said, pausing, making a face like she was thinking, then said, "No, I still want to do it," she continued.

Zarblerg vanished, then reappeared, holding another large sack.

She emptied the sack containing bat hairs, mercuric-nitric acid crystals, and mandrake roots into the fountain. The huge quantity was Hieronymus' entire stock of the items.

Next, Millicent uttered a few words of power and pointed toward the fountain, sending out a spout of fire that engulfed it.

She began the demon-summoning incantation, and all was silent except for some whimpering from the prisoners praying to the moons.

When she finished, the room became very still and suddenly so cold that frost appeared everywhere there was glass. Most of the light seemed to become sucked out of the room, and an inky darkness grew in the center of the magic circle. The quiet was deafening.

Zarblerg whined and cowered behind its Mistress.

Lamashtu looked on with a kind of reverence.

The mages backed away and ran, their faces marked with fear, escaping through the servants' exit. The other demons followed their masters.

A terrible, powerful presence could be felt, and a figure began to form above the fountain and slowly coalesce. As it consolidated, a male figure took shape, but it was twice the height of a normal man. Its face looked human, indeed handsome, except it had short horns protruding from its head. Its eyes blazed pure evil, and the thin lips of its mouth bore an unspeakable cruelty.

Lamashtu got down to a knee and cast her head down.

Zarblerg was prostrate on the floor, whining, not daring to look.

"Who dares summon the prince of all demons?" It had a normal human voice, at once both beautiful in tone yet also unspeakably cold, utterly devoid of emotion except hate.

"Millicent of the House of Ravens, daughter of Lucian, former Minister of Magic of Rathberg." She said, keeping her voice unwavering only with great effort.

The Prince slowly turned to her.

She tried to avoid looking it in the eyes but felt compelled to do so.

"Why have you summoned me, daughter of Lucian?"

"These men did great evil to me and my city, and I offer you their souls. They are the most powerful men in the city, Ministers and Directors."

"I will take these souls with gratitude; they will serve me for eternity and be my playthings."

The prisoners looked mad with terror, but none of them could move. The demon languidly approached each one in turn and strangled them with a single hand. Millicent watched it take Aldebrand and felt an almost sexual elation.

After it was over, the demon turned back to Millicent, "Your act of revenge pleases me. But I am not satisfied. I will take your soul, then spend some time on this plane, wrecking carnage."

"Spare me, Prince. I will serve you," Millicent begged, terrified and stunned at this turn of events.

"Indeed, you will serve me for eternity." The Prince began to walk towards her.

She couldn't move; she was not exactly paralyzed; it was as if she could not muster the will to move her legs. The Arch-demon was only steps away, and Millicent was terrified. She found that she could still move her arms slightly if she concentrated. Her only hope was to use the second crystal she created for the Ten Thousand Elephants spell. With a supreme effort of will, she was able to reach into her coat pocket and take out the crystal, letting it drop to the floor. It broke, and immediately, she felt its magic released. Surprised, the Arch-demon paused for a moment and looked around as the rumbling began, at first very low. That interruption was enough for the demon's paralysis spell to be broken, and she was able to run for the exit, Zarblerg scrambling away on her heels. By the time she had run three steps, the tower was already beginning to fall. Great chunks of stone were falling all around her.

She was not going to make it out of the building in time.

Being crushed under the tower was preferable to being taken to the underworld to be the slave of the demon Prince was her last thought of consolation before oblivion.

An indeterminate amount of time later, she woke in great pain and in total darkness. She heard Zarblerg calling to her, "Mistress! Mistress, wake up!" He was very close.

"Moons Zarblerg, your breath stinks."

She felt like she was trapped under a great weight, yet it seemed soft, like a giant pillow.

"I was able to protect you from the falling rubble with my body, Mistress, but we are trapped. If I go back to my plane, there will be a cavity for you, but I fear more rubble may fall."

"There's no choice, Zar. We have to try, but I can't breathe. Leave this plane and re-materialize outside the rubble; try to dig me out."

"Mistress."

All of a sudden, the pressure on her body was

released, but then she heard some rubble settling, and something fell on her leg, and she blacked out again. She woke but was in terrible agony. Her stomach hurt, and she still had great trouble breathing. If she tried to inhale deeply, she felt a horrible sharp pain and had to exhale immediately. She tried short, shallow breathing, but it was not enough, and she felt lightheaded; she knew she was severely broken inside. "Zarblerg," she called.

The pressure returned suddenly as Zarblerg re-materialized on top of her. She fought off unconsciousness. "Go to my castle, find the healing potion in the kitchen. Bring it. Hurry!"

Again, he was gone.

She touched her head and felt a gaping wound and flowing blood. The pain was unbearable. With each passing second, she could feel her life force slowly draining away and knew death was near. She blacked out, then, as if in a dream, felt a burning liquid in her mouth and throat. After that, oblivion.

She was trapped in an unending nightmare of pain and fever dreams. Her room at Bedlam, nurses who were demons torturing her, falling, Benedict laughing at her like a madman, the Prince of Demons approaching and her unable to move, Regina lying in a pool of blood, her mother far away beckoning to her, her father on the electric chair, drowned men chasing her down the city streets. She spent 100 lifetimes in the dream.

CHAPTER 84

Millicent woke in a bed in a small room, alone. Her leg was in a cast and elevated. Her head was wrapped in bandages. Wiggling her toes and fingers, she was otherwise intact except for a terrible headache. Was she in prison? She sensed no spell dampeners. No guards that she could see or restraints; that was a good sign. By the blue and white stripes painted on the walls, she could tell it was a hospital in the Tower of Healing. She remembered nothing after throwing the Ten Thousand Elephants spell and running for the exit.

"Zarblerg," she called out weakly.

He appeared, seemingly undamaged.

"What happened?"

"Mistress?"

"After I cast the earthquake spell, what happened? I don't remember," she croaked. Her mouth was so dry.

"When you threw the crystal down, the tower began to shake and fall. The arch demon was distracted and we were free to move again. We ran, but before you made it to safety, a great stone was about to fall on you, so I knocked you down and covered you with my body. You were unconscious but woke and told me to bring you the healing potion. When I returned, you were in the place between worlds. I poured the potion into your mouth, and you returned but were still very damaged. I dematerialized outside, but I was too injured to dig you out, so I tried to find people to help, but they were afraid and ran from me, so I consumed them and was able to heal quickly. After a time, I was able to start digging you out.

"What happened with the arch demon? Was it destroyed?"

"No, Mistress, it returned to the other plane when the tower fell, but it was very angry."

"I imagine so."

"What will it do? Will it try to kill me?" she asked.

"It can only come to this plane if summoned, but it hates you and will never forget."

"That's grand. An evil arch demon hates me and wants revenge. What happened to the other mages?"

"I don't know, Mistress."

"Find Balthazar and bring him to me."

"Mistress." Zarblerg disappeared.

The nurse entered and seemed genuinely pleased that she was awake. Millicent was given water and drank eagerly. She asked for a mirror and was mortified at her gaunt appearance and unwashed hair, so she cast a glamour spell on herself.

An hour later, Balthazar appeared, smiling. "We thought you were dead, crushed under the towers, or worse, taken by the arch demon."

"I thought I was dead too. What's happening out there in the city?"

"We were able to subdue what was left of the resistance from the Justice Ministry; they are in Nightstone Prison now. The previous inmates were pardoned. We culled the rest of the traitors from the Magic Ministry, and now it is staffed by former prison inmates, and I was elected Minister. The city is in chaos, but we will soon restore order with the wisdom of the Ministry. Our first order of business is to outlaw Galvanism."

"Congratulations. I wish I could be out there to help."

"Don't worry, we have it in command. You stay here and heal, and don't worry, you will not be punished for any of your actions."

"Punished? For what?"

Still smiling, Balthazar said, "Destroying a good part of the city, summoning an arch demon, not to mention all the innocent killings."

"Oh, that."

"There is a faction of elders who want you

imprisoned or banished, but I should be able to smooth things over. You did free us from the tyranny of the Justice and Tech Ministries after all."

I never really thought about what would happen when it was all over, she thought to herself. She had imagined a city in ruins and just walking away, back to Rabe Hold.

"Come see me after you have healed and we will talk," he said as he left the room.

CHAPTER 85

Benedict came to Millicent her the next day. To her surprise, he brought a bouquet of flowers.

"Thank you," she said earnestly, and he put the flowers on a table.

"You're quite welcome. So, the Ophidian Tower and the other towers surrounding it are destroyed. All that is left of the Justice Ministry are some low-level clerks and secretaries. The dam is destroyed, and most of the docks are flooded out. Most of the Tech Ministry are dead or in prison. There is no more electricity in the city, and Galvanism is not mentioned on the streets. Did everything go to plan?"

"You forgot to mention the people at the gala that I sent to Hell," she said, smirking sweetly.

"To hell? I gather you mean that literally," he said with eyebrows raised," Of course you do. Actually, I'm not surprised."

She smiled, "So, I imagine you will be wanting your payment."

"Well, it was agreed."

"Go to my estate. In my desk, you will find the deed. Bring it here and I will sign it over to you. It's worth much more than I owe you."

He smiled and bowed gallantly.

Her smile faded as she contemplated his question: Was it all worth Regina's life? She could not decide, in all honesty, but she had a sense that everything that happened was inevitable, predestined.

In a few weeks, she had healed enough to walk again and strolled into the city. Rathberg was abuzz with activity. The area around the Ophidian Tower had been cleared, and new construction had begun. By order of the Magic Ministry, electric wires had been completely removed from the city along with all other traces of the Galvanist machinery.

She went to the Magic Ministry Tower to see Minister Balthazar. Things looked the same, although perhaps fewer people. Casting a spell, she floated gently to the top floor and entered the Minister's office.

"Minister Balthazar," she said, smiling.

"Millicent. I have good news, I have smoothed things over with the Council of Elders, you will not be banished, and I even convinced them to give you a position in the Ministry."

"Really? A female, in the Ministry," she said ironically.

"A few even nominated you to be Minister. You

have proven your skill with magic, and you do have the pedigree. Your age was an issue, but I was able to convince enough of the Council to promise their vote for Secretary."

She sat down and sighed. "Thank you, Balthazar, but I am tired of the city. I wish to go back to my castle and live quietly for a while."

"Ah. Understandable. Well, if you should change your mind."

Before leaving the city, Millicent visited Regina's grave. Upon reaching the grave, she knelt down, feeling the cool, damp earth beneath her. Tenderly, she arranged the flowers; pansies – Regina's favorite, the vibrant purple contrasting against the muted gray of the gravestone. She took the lotus position and meditated the way Regina had taught her, immersing herself in the tranquil atmosphere. Finally, with a heavy heart, she whispered her goodbye. As she departed from the cemetery, a raven alighted on a nearby tree, its gaze following her with solemn intent. She thought back to the day of the coup, when she invaded the stranger's funeral and felt ashamed at her immature behavior.

CHAPTER 86

A splendid four-horse carriage glided through the gatehouse into Rabe Hold. Out stepped Millicent, dressed in a fine gown of blue silk cut scandalously above the knee. Following her were three young female servants, all gazing up at the keep with wide eyes. No longer would the mysterious Countess Arabella haunt the castle alone; she was gone, and instead, her niece Millicent would take up residence and perhaps even invite some of the villagers over for social calls. Her intention was clear: to reside quietly away from the bustling city and study magic. She ordered the driver to begin unloading the baggage.

The first week went quietly, and Millicent and the staff had settled into a comfortable routine. Zarblerg was given orders to not be seen by the servants, to prevent them from fleeing in terror. She hired a crew of masons to resume the restoration of the castle. No more hasty work by her demon; these workers would do the job skillfully.

Then, one morning, a piercing shrieking woke Millicent from a sound sleep, and she jumped out of bed. Looking out her window into the dawn-lit courtyard, she saw a baby wyvern, obviously injured and in pain.

She ran down to the courtyard in her nightgown and bare feet. "Shh, little one, let me help you." She crouched down and coaxed the animal to be still. Gently, she touched its broken wing and cast a healing spell. Immediately, the wyvern stopped fussing and stood up. It faced her, uttered a small chirp, and took flight, doing a little circle above Millicent before departing.

Several days later, at dusk, she was reading in her study and heard the chirp of a wyvern from outside. It had landed in the courtyard on the statue of a raven, which she had recently commissioned.

"Well, hello again," she called to it from her window. "Wait there."

She ran to the kitchen and grabbed some leftover goat, then ran to the courtyard and held it up to the wyvern so it could see. It cocked its head curiously, and she threw the meal down on the ground. It jumped down from the statue and gobbled it up unceremoniously.

She came a little closer, and it held still, not frightened.

Just then, Zarblerg appeared and, with a squeal, suddenly lunged for the creature.

"No Zarblerg!" She jumped between the demon and the wyvern, which tried to take flight but was so startled it fell over.

"Go away, and don't come back until I summon you!" she said, furious.

"Mistress." he sounded angry, but she didn't notice as she comforted the frightened creature.

"What should I call you? I think you are a girl, no?" She pondered. "I know, I'll call you Flayre. We are going to be great friends, I think."

Millicent of the House of Ravens – Spoiled daughter of Lucian

Lucian – Millicent's father, Minister of Magic

Pythomon – Lucian's demon

Annabelle – Millicent's mother that died when she was an infant

Beatrix – Millicent's elderly aunt

Zarblerg – Millicent's Demon

Cerberus – The Doorman to Millicent's building

Nicodemus – Millicent's elderly magic tutor.

Colette – Millicent's brunette alter ego that she uses while visiting the village incognito

Claudette – Millicent's alias when she returns to Rathburg

Arabella – The name of the imaginary countess who owns the castle

Hieronymus – Old man who works in the Apothecary shop

Aldebrand – Director in the Ministry of Justice, promoted to Minister

Gumarich – Aldebrand's assistant

Morcant – Justice Minister

Loque – Minister of Trade

Petrina – Millicent's friend, her age

Benedict – Millicent's fencing instructor

Aldous – Elderly blind magician in the catacombs

Adramalech – Aldous' demon

Tranton – Minister of Tech

Cynebald – Tech technician

Gonagas – The raven figurine, from the Chuktuk sect

Theobald – Crazy old man that is squatting in the castle

Lucinda the Red – Madam of a whorehouse

Sabina, Isabetta, Ava – Bedlam inmates

Donal – A Bedlam guard they blackmail

Regina – Witch, niece of Theobald.

Archibald – Bailiff

Baron Pim – Lives in an estate in the country

Inspector Quentin – Officer in the Justice Ministry

Balthazar – Second in command (director) to her father. Demon named Albramonethsah

Phineas – Slender mage with pigeon who can kill with a look named Shedim

Severin – Aristocratic mage with a demon named Lamashtu

Malthus – Mage with a demon named Asgoth

About the Author

Jon Fabris was born and grew up in the suburbs of Boston during the Brady Bunch era of the 70's. He graduated from Bentley College in Waltham Massachusetts with a computer degree. Presently he lives in rural North Carolina, in a Civil War era farmhouse, next to a log cabin he restored by himself, and in his front yard is a 40 foot pirate ship. In addition to being a sought after computer programmer, he is also a skilled sculptor, potter, animator, woodworker, builder, game designer, filmmaker, and writer.

Sign up for the mailing list for occasional (no more than once a month) updates.
https://jon-fabris-author.mailchimpsites.com/

If you enjoyed reading this novel, please leave a review on Amazon. Reviews are very important to new writers and are very appreciated.

Link to review:

www.amazon.com/review/create-review/?asin=B0DHQPTTGY

Other books by Jon Fabris:

The Enchanted Village

A dark but humorous fantasy novel brimming with heroes, knights, witches, elves, dwarfs, goblins, trolls, giants, ogres, dragons, and unicorns. The book takes inspiration from the darker tales of the Brothers Grimm with a dash of Midsummer Night's Dream.

Most of the adventure takes place in the secluded village of Bunwych, a town drenched in magic due to its proximity to the fairy land of Elfhame.

The main protagonist is a woman; strong but conflicted, trying her best to raise her children alone. The chief antagonist is the Fairy Queen, who hates the humans and attempts to meddle with their affairs. A mysterious knight from the distant, more civilized part of the kingdom arrives and attempts to purge the haunted ruined castle of its ghosts. Comic relief is provided by the bumbling Dwarf King who, after killing his fiance for mentioning fairies and flowers, undertakes to woo the most beautiful girl in Bunwych. The characters move through a series of adventures building to the climax on midsummer's night.

Inside the book are 22 charming full color illustrations.

Tales from the Age of Legends

Tales from the Age of Legends is a collection of 22 short stories, set in a mythical period when magic was commonplace, vampires and other monsters roamed the land, ghosts tormented their murderers, and wizards and witches were potent and feared. Combining the brisk pace and action of Robert E. Howard, the diabolical horror of Poe, the romance and intrigue of a gothic mystery novel, the surprise twists of an O Henry story, the humor of Twain, the enchantment of fairy tales, the exotic wonder of the Arabian Nights, along with a smattering of steampunk, this book is a stew of heroic and dark fantasy. The stories are woven together by a traveling storyteller named Barret, a monastic educated scribe and adventurer who is also the chief protagonist in some of the tales.

Available on Amazon in ebook and paperback formats.

www.ingramcontent.com/pod-product-compliance
Lightning Source LLC
Chambersburg PA
CBHW061926170626
46813CB00006B/2315